"You can't play these kinds of games. You don't know the rules."

"I don't know what your problem is. You don't want me, so what do you care if they do?"

"Hayley, honey, I don't *want* to want you, but that is not the same thing as not wanting you. It is not even close. What I want is something you can't handle."

She tilted her head to the side, her hair falling over her shoulder like a glossy curtain. "Maybe I want to be shocked. Maybe I want something I'm not quite ready for."

"No," he said, his tone emphatic now. "You're on a big kick to have experiences. But there are much nicer men you can have experiences with."

She bared her teeth. "I was trying! You just scared them off."

"You're not having experiences with those clowns. They wouldn't know how to handle a woman if she came with an instruction manual. And let me tell you, women do not come with an instruction manual. You just have to know what to do."

"And you know what to do?"

"Damn straight," he returned.

"So," she said, tilting her chin up, looking stubborn. "Show me."

* * *

Seduce Me, Cowboy is part of *New York Times* bestselling author Maisey Yates's

Copper Ridge series.

Dear Reader,

I'm pleased to welcome you back to Copper Ridge, Oregon! Home of mountains, the ocean and, of course... cowboys. Jonathan Bear and Hayley Thompson are two characters I knew I wanted to write for quite some time.

I knew Jonathan was going to be a tough nut to crack. When I wrote his sister Rebecca's book, *Last Chance Rebel*, I knew it would take a special heroine to deal with him. As for Hayley, well, I thought I just needed to find the right man for sweet Hayley, the pastor's daughter and younger sister of the town's favorite bartender, Ace, who got his happily-ever-after in *One Night Charmer*.

But of course that wasn't the case.

You see, Hayley has been good all of her life. What Hayley needed...well, what Hayley needed was the wrong man. And Jonathan is definitely the wrong man for her. The taciturn rancher is too old, too hard, too experienced...and way too much her boss. But attraction doesn't follow logic, as Jonathan and Hayley discover, and soon these two people who are all wrong for each other are finding out that somehow it all feels right.

Jonathan and Hayley are truly a match made in Copper Ridge, and it was a joy to write their story and give them their happy ending.

I hope you enjoy it as much as I did.

Happy Reading!

Maisey

MAISEY YATES

———

SEDUCE ME, COWBOY

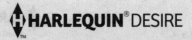

HARLEQUIN® DESIRE

Recycling programs
for this product may
not exist in your area.

ISBN-13: 978-0-373-83830-1

Seduce Me, Cowboy

Printed in U.S.A.

Maisey Yates is a *New York Times* bestselling author of more than thirty romance novels. She has a coffee habit she has no interest in kicking and a slight Pinterest addiction. She lives with her husband and children in the Pacific Northwest. When Maisey isn't writing, she can be found singing in the grocery store, shopping for shoes online and probably not doing dishes. Check out her website, maiseyyates.com.

Books by Maisey Yates

Harlequin Desire

Copper Ridge

Take Me, Cowboy
Hold Me, Cowboy
Seduce Me, Cowboy

HQN Books

Copper Ridge

Shoulda Been a Cowboy
Part Time Cowboy
Brokedown Cowboy
Bad News Cowboy
A Copper Ridge Christmas
One Night Charmer

Harlequin Presents

Bound to the Warrior King
His Diamond of Convenience
One Night to Risk It All
His Ring Is Not Enough
A Game of Vows

Visit her Author Profile page on Harlequin.com, or maiseyyates.com, for more titles!

To the whole Harlequin team.
This is the best job ever.
Thank you for letting me do it.

One

Hayley Thompson was a good girl. In all the ways that phrase applied. The kind of girl every mother wished her son would bring home for Sunday dinner.

Of course, the mothers of Copper Ridge were much more enthusiastic about Hayley than their sons were, but that had never been a problem. She had never really tried dating, anyway. Dates were the least of her problems.

She was more worried about the constant feeling that she was under a microscope. That she was a trained seal, sitting behind the desk in the church office exactly as one might expect from a small-town pastor's daughter—who also happened to be the church secretary.

And what did she have to show for being so good? Absolutely nothing.

Meanwhile, her older brother had gone out into the world and done whatever he wanted. He'd broken every rule. Run away from home. Gotten married, gotten divorced. Come back home and opened a bar in the same town where his father preached sermons. All while Hayley had stayed and behaved herself. Done everything that was expected of her.

Ace was the prodigal son. He hadn't just received forgiveness for his transgressions. He'd been rewarded. He had so many things well-behaved Hayley wanted and didn't have.

He'd found love again in his wife, Sierra. They had children. The doting attention of Hayley's parents—a side effect of being the first to supply grandchildren, she felt—while Hayley had…

Well, nothing.

Nothing but a future as a very well-behaved spinster.

That was why she was here now. Clutching a newspaper in her hand until it was wrinkled tight. She hadn't even known people still put ads in the paper for job listings, but while she'd been sitting in The Grind yesterday on Copper Ridge's main street, watching people go by and feeling a strange sense of being untethered, she'd grabbed the local paper.

That had led her to the job listings. And seeing

as she was unemployed for the first time since she was sixteen years old, she'd read them.

Every single one of them had been submitted by people she knew. Businesses she'd grown up patronizing, or businesses owned by people she knew from her dad's congregation. And if she got a job somewhere like that, she might as well have stayed on at the church.

Except for one listing. Assistant to Jonathan Bear, owner of Gray Bear Construction. The job was for him personally, but would also entail clerical work for his company and some work around his home.

She didn't know anything about the company. She'd never had a house built, after all. Neither had her mother and father. And she'd never heard his name before, and was reasonably sure she'd never seen him at church.

She wanted that distance.

Familiar, nagging guilt gnawed at the edges of her heart. Her parents were good people. They loved her very much. And she loved them. But she felt like a beloved goldfish. With people watching her every move and tapping on the glass. Plus, the bowl was restricting, when she was well aware there was an entire ocean out there.

Step one in her plan for independence had been to acquire her own apartment. Cassie Caldwell, owner of The Grind, and her husband, Jake, had moved out of the space above the coffee shop a while ago.

Happily, it had been vacant and ready to rent, and Hayley had taken advantage of that. So, with the money she'd saved up, she'd moved into that place. And then, after hoarding a few months' worth of rent, she had finally worked up the courage to quit.

Her father had been... She wouldn't go so far as to say he'd been disappointed. John Thompson never had a harsh word for anyone. He was all kind eyes and deep conviction. The type of goodness Hayley could only marvel at, that made her feel as though she could never quite measure up.

But she could tell her father had been confused. And she hadn't been able to explain herself, not fully. Because she didn't want either of her parents to know that ultimately, this little journey of independence would lead straight out of Copper Ridge.

She had to get out of the fishbowl. She needed people to stop tapping on her glass.

Virtue wasn't its own reward. For years she'd believed it would be. But then...suddenly, watching Ace at the dinner table at her parents' house, with his family, she'd realized the strange knot in her stomach wasn't anger over his abandonment, over the way he'd embarrassed their parents with his behavior.

It was envy.

Envy of all he had, of his freedom. Well, this was her chance to have some of that for herself, and she couldn't do it with everyone watching.

She took a deep breath and regarded the house in

front of her. If she didn't know it was the home and office of the owner of Gray Bear Construction, she would be tempted to assume it was some kind of resort.

The expansive front porch was made entirely out of logs, stained with a glossy, honey-colored sheen that caught the light and made the place look like it was glowing. The green metal roof was designed to withstand harsh weather—which down in town by the beach wasn't much of an issue. But a few miles inland, here in the mountains, she could imagine there was snow in winter.

She wondered if she would need chains for her car. But she supposed she'd cross that bridge when she came to it. It was early spring, and she didn't even have the job yet.

Getting the job, and keeping it through winter, was only a pipe dream at this point.

She took a deep breath and started up the path, the bark-laden ground soft beneath her feet. She inhaled deeply, the sharp scent of pine filling her lungs. It was cool beneath the trees, and she wrapped her arms around herself as she walked up the steps and made her way to the front door.

She knocked before she had a chance to rethink her actions, and then she waited.

She was just about to knock again when she heard footsteps. She quickly put her hand down at her side. Then lifted it again, brushing her hair out of her face. Then she clasped her hands in front of her, then put them back at her sides again. Then she decided to hold them in front of her again.

She had just settled on that position when the door jerked open.

She had rehearsed her opening remarks. Had practiced making a natural smile in the mirror—which was easy after so many years manning the front desk of a church—but all that disappeared completely when she looked at the man standing in front of her.

He was... Well, he was nothing like she'd expected, which left her grappling for what exactly she had been expecting. Somebody older. Certainly not somebody who towered over her like a redwood.

Jonathan Bear wasn't someone you could anticipate.

His dark, glittering eyes assessed her; his mouth pressed into a thin line. His black hair was tied back, but it was impossible for her to tell just how long it was from where she stood.

"Who are you?" he asked, his tone uncompromising.

"I'm here to interview for the assistant position. Were you expecting someone else?" Her stomach twisted with anxiety. He wasn't what she had expected, and now she was wondering if she was what *he* had expected. Maybe he wanted somebody older, with more qualifications. Or somebody more... Well, sexy secretary than former church secretary.

Though, she looked very nice in this twin set and pencil skirt, if she said so herself.

"No," he said, moving away from the door. "Come in."

"Oh," she said, scampering to follow his direction.

"The office is upstairs," he said, taking great strides through the entryway and heading toward a massive curved staircase.

She found herself taking very quick steps to try and keep up with him. And it was difficult to do that when she was distracted by the beauty of the house. She was trying to take in all the details as she trailed behind him up the stairs, her low heels clicking on the hardwood.

"I'm Hayley Thompson," she said, "which I know the résumé said, but you didn't know who I was... So..."

"We're the only two people here," he said, looking back at her, lifting one dark brow. "So knowing your name isn't really that important, is it?"

She couldn't tell if he was joking. She laughed nervously, and it got her no response at all. So then she was concerned she had miscalculated.

They reached the top of the stairs, and she followed him down a long hallway, the sound of her steps dampened now by a long carpet runner the colors of the nature that surrounded them. Brown, forest green and a red that reminded her of cranberries.

The house smelled new. Which was maybe a

strange observation to make, but the scent of wood lingered in the air, and something that reminded her of paint.

"How long have you lived here?" she asked, more comfortable with polite conversation than contending with silence.

"Just moved in last month," he said. "One of our designs. You might have guessed, this is what Gray Bear does. Custom homes. That's our specialty. And since my construction company merged with Grayson Design, we're doing design as well as construction."

"How many people can buy places like this?" she asked, turning in a circle while she walked, daunted by the amount of house they had left behind them, and the amount that was still before them.

"You would be surprised. For a lot of our clients these are only vacation homes. Escapes to the coast and to the mountains. Mostly, we work on the Oregon coast, but we make exceptions for some of the higher-paying clientele."

"That's…kind of amazing. I mean, something of this scale right here in Copper Ridge. Or I guess, technically, we're outside the city limits."

"Still the same zip code," he said, lifting a shoulder.

He took hold of two sliding double doors fashioned to look like barn doors and slid them open, revealing a huge office space with floor-to-ceiling windows and a view that made her jaw drop.

The sheer immensity of the mountains spread before them was incredible on its own. But beyond that, she could make out the faint gray of the ocean, white-capped waves and jagged rocks rising out of the surf.

"The best of everything," he said. "Sky, mountains, ocean. That kind of sums up the company. Now that you know about us, you can tell me why I should hire you."

"I want the job," she said, her tone hesitant. As soon as she said the words, she realized how ridiculous they were. Everybody who interviewed for this position would want the job. "I was working as a secretary for my father's…business," she said, feeling guilty about fudging a little bit on her résumé. But she hadn't really wanted to say she was working at her father's church, because… Well, she just wanted to come in at a slightly more neutral position.

"You were working for your family?"

"Yes," she said.

He crossed his arms, and she felt slightly intimidated. He was the largest man she'd ever seen. At least, he felt large. Something about all the height and muscles and presence combined.

"We're going to have to get one thing straight right now, Hayley. I'm not your daddy. So if you're used to a kind and gentle working environment where you get a lot of chances because firing you would make it awkward around the holidays, this might take some adjustment for you. I'm damned hard to please. And

I'm not a very nice boss. There's a lot of work to do around here. I hate paperwork, and I don't want to have to do any form twice. If you make mistakes and I have to sit at that desk longer as a result, you're fired. If I've hired you to make things easier between myself and my clients, and something you do makes it harder, you're fired. If you pass on a call to me that I shouldn't have to take, you're fired."

She nodded, wishing she had a notepad, not because she was ever going to forget what he'd said, but so she could underscore the fact that she was paying attention. "Anything else?"

"Yeah," he said, a slight smile curving his lips. "You're also fired if you fuck up my coffee."

This was a mistake. Jonathan Bear was absolutely certain of it. But he had earned millions making mistakes, so what was one more? Nobody else had responded to his ad.

Except for this pale, strange little creature who looked barely twenty and wore the outfit of an eighty-year-old woman.

She was… Well, she wasn't the kind of formidable woman who could stand up to the rigors of working with him.

His sister, Rebecca, would say—with absolutely no tact at all—that he sucked as a boss. And maybe she was right, but he didn't really care. He was busy, and right now he hated most of what he was busy with.

There was irony in that, he knew. He had worked hard all his life. While a lot of his friends had sought solace and oblivion in drugs and alcohol, Jonathan had figured it was best to sweat the poison right out.

He'd gotten a job on a construction site when he was fifteen, and learned his trade. He'd gotten to where he was faster, better than most of the men around him. By the time he was twenty, he had been doing serious custom work on the more upscale custom homes he'd built with West Construction.

But he wanted more. There was a cap on what he could make with that company, and he didn't like a ceiling. He wanted open skies and the freedom to go as high, as fast as he wanted. So he could amass so much it could never be taken from him.

So he'd risked striking out on his own. No one had believed a kid from the wrong side of the tracks could compete with West. But Jonathan had courted business across city and county lines. And created a reputation beyond Copper Ridge so that when people came looking to build retirement homes or vacation properties, his was the name they knew.

He had built everything he had, brick by brick. In a strictly literal sense in some cases.

And every brick built a stronger wall against all the things he had left behind. Poverty, uncertainty, the lack of respect paid to a man in his circumstances.

Then six months ago, Joshua Grayson had approached him. Originally from Copper Ridge, the man had been looking for a foothold back in town after years in Seattle. Faith Grayson, Joshua's sister was quickly becoming the most sought after architect in the Pacific Northwest. But the siblings had decided it was time to bring the business back home in order to be closer to their parents.

And so Joshua asked Jonathan if he would consider bringing design in-house, making Bear Construction into Gray Bear.

This gave Jonathan reach into urban areas, into Seattle. Had him managing remote crews and dealing with many projects at one time. And it had pushed him straight out of the building game in many ways. He had turned into a desk drone. And while his bank account had grown astronomically, he was quite a ways from the life he thought he'd live after reaching this point.

Except the house. The house was finally finished. Finally, he was living in one of the places he'd built.

Finally, Jonathan Bear, that poor Indian kid who wasn't worth anything to anyone, bastard son of the biggest bastard in town, had his house on the side of the mountain and more money than he would ever be able to spend.

And he was bored out of his mind.

Boredom, it turned out, worked him into a hell of a temper. He had a feeling Hayley Thompson wasn't strong enough to stand up to that. But he expected to go through a few assistants before he found one who could handle it. She might as well be number one.

"You've got the job," he said. "You can start tomorrow."

Her eyes widened, and he noticed they were a strange shade of blue. Gray in some lights, shot through with a dark, velvet navy that reminded him of the ocean before a storm. It made him wonder if there was some hidden strength there.

They would both find out.

"I got the job? Just like that?"

"Getting the job was always going to be the easy part. It's keeping the job that might be tricky. My list of reasons to hire you are short—you showed up. The list of reasons I have for why I might fire you is much longer."

"You're not very reassuring," she said, her lips tilting down in a slight frown.

He laughed. "If you want to go back and work for your daddy, do that. I'm not going to call you. But maybe you'll appreciate my ways later. Other jobs will seem easy after this one."

She just looked at him, her jaw firmly set, her petite body rigid with determination. "What time do you want me here?"

"Seven o'clock. Don't be late. Or else…"

"You'll fire me. I've got the theme."

"Excellent. Hayley Thompson, you've got yourself a job."

Two

Hayley scrubbed her face as she walked into The Grind through the private entrance from her upstairs apartment. It was early. But she wanted to make sure she wasn't late to work.

On account of all the firing talk.

"Good morning," Cassie said from behind the counter, smiling cheerfully. Hayley wondered if Cassie was really thrilled to be at work this early in the morning. Hayley knew all about presenting a cheerful face to anyone who might walk in the door.

You couldn't have a bad day when you worked at the church.

"I need coffee," Hayley said, not bothering to

force a grin. She wasn't at work yet. She paused. "Do you know Jonathan Bear?"

Cassie gave her a questioning look. "Yes, I'm friends with his sister, Rebecca. She owns the store across the street."

"Right," Hayley said, frowning. "I don't think I've ever met her. But I've seen her around town."

Hayley was a few years younger than Cassie, and probably a bit younger than Rebecca, as well, which meant they had never been in classes together at school, and had never shared groups of friends. Not that Hayley had much in the way of friends. People tended to fear the pastor's daughter would put a damper on things.

No one had tested the theory.

"So yes, I know Jonathan in passing. He's… Well, he's not very friendly." Cassie laughed. "Why?"

"He just hired me."

Cassie's expression contorted into one of horror and Hayley saw her start to backpedal. "He's probably fine. It's just that he's very protective of Rebecca because he raised her, you know, and all that. And she had her accident, and had to have a lot of medical procedures done… So my perception of him is based entirely on that. I'm sure he's a great boss."

"No," Hayley said, "you were right the first time. He's a grumpy cuss. Do you have any idea what kind of coffee he drinks?"

Cassie frowned, a small notch appearing between

her brows. "He doesn't come in that often. But when he does I think he gets a dark roast, large, black, no sugar, with a double shot of espresso."

"How do you remember that?"

"It's my job. And there are a lot of people I know by drink and not by name."

"Well, I will take one of those for him. And hope that it's still hot by the time I get up the mountain."

"Okay. And a coffee for you with room for cream?"

"Yes," Hayley said. "I don't consider my morning caffeination ritual a punishment like some people seem to."

"Hey," Cassie said, "some people just like their coffee unadulterated. But I am not one of them. I feel you."

Hayley paid for her order and made her way to the back of the store, looking around at the warm, quaint surroundings. Locals had filed in and were filling up the tables, reading their papers, opening laptops and dropping off bags and coats to secure the coveted positions in the tiny coffee shop.

Then a line began to form, and Hayley was grateful she had come as early as she had.

A moment later, her order was ready. Popping the lid off her cup at the cream and sugar station, she gave herself a generous helping of both. She walked back out the way she had come in, going to her car, which was parked behind the building in her reserved space.

She got inside, wishing she'd warmed up the vehicle before placing her order. It wasn't too cold this morning, but she could see her breath in the damp air. She positioned both cups of coffee in the cup holders of her old Civic, and then headed to the main road, which was void of traffic—and would remain that way for the entire day.

She liked the pace of Copper Ridge, she really did. Liked the fact that she knew so many people, that people waved and smiled when she walked by. Liked that there were no traffic lights, and that you rarely had to wait for more than one car at a four-way stop.

She loved the mountains, and she loved the ocean.

But she knew there were things beyond this place, too. And she wanted to see them.

Needed to see them.

She thought about all those places as she drove along the winding road to Jonathan Bear's house. She had the vague thought that if she went to London or Paris, if she looked at the Eiffel Tower or Big Ben, structures so old and lasting—structures that had been there for centuries—maybe she would learn something about herself.

Maybe she would find what she couldn't identify here. Maybe she would find the cure for the elusive ache in her chest when she saw Ace with Sierra and their kids.

Would find the freedom to be herself—whoever

that might be. To flirt and date, and maybe drink a beer. To escape the confines that so rigidly held her.

Even driving out of town this morning, instead of to the church, was strange. Usually, she felt as though she were moving through the grooves of a well-worn track. There were certain places she went in town— her parents' home, the church, the grocery store, The Grind, her brother's brewery and restaurant, but never his bar—and she rarely deviated from that routine.

She supposed this drive would become routine soon enough.

She pulled up to the front of the house, experiencing a sharp sense of déjà vu as she walked up to the front porch to knock again. Except this time her stomach twisted with an even greater sense of trepidation. Not because Jonathan Bear was an unknown, but because she knew a little bit about him now. And what she knew terrified her.

The door jerked open before she could pound against it. "Just come in next time," he said.

"Oh."

"During business hours. I was expecting you."

"Expecting me to be late?" she asked, holding out his cup of coffee.

He arched a dark brow. "Maybe." He tilted his head to the side. "What's that?"

"Probably coffee." She didn't know why she was being anything other than straightforward and sweet. He'd made it very clear that he had exacting standards. Likely, he wanted his assistant to fulfill his every whim before it even occurred to him, and to do so with a smile. Likely, he didn't want his assistant to sass him, even lightly.

Except, something niggled at her, telling her he wouldn't respect her at all if she acted like a doormat. She was good at reading people. It was a happy side effect of being quiet. Of having few friends, of being an observer. Of spending years behind the church desk, not sure who might walk through the door seeking help. That experience had taught Hayley not only kindness, but also discernment.

And that was why she chose to follow her instincts with Jonathan.

"It's probably coffee?" he asked, taking the cup from her, anyway.

"Yes," she returned. "Probably."

He turned away from her, heading toward the stairs, but she noticed that he took the lid off the cup and examined the contents. She smiled as she followed him up the stairs to the office.

The doors were already open, the computer that faced the windows fired up. There were papers everywhere. And pens sat across nearly every surface.

"Why so many pens?" she asked.

"If I have to stop and look for one I waste an awful lot of time cussing."

"Fair enough."

"I have to go outside and take care of the horses,

but I want you to go through that stack of invoices and enter all the information into the spreadsheet on the computer. Can you do that?"

"Spreadsheets are my specialty. You have horses?"

He nodded. "This is kind of a ranch."

"Oh," she said. "I didn't realize."

"No reason you should." Then he turned, grabbing a black cowboy hat off a hook and putting it firmly on his head. "I'll be back in a couple of hours. And I'm going to want more coffee. The machine is downstairs in the kitchen. Should be pretty easy. Probably."

Then he brushed his fingertips against the brim of his hat, nodding slightly before walking out, leaving her alone.

When he left, something in her chest loosened, eased. She hadn't realized just how tense she'd felt in his presence.

She took a deep breath, sitting down at the desk in front of the computer, eyeing the healthy stack of papers to her left. Then she looked over the monitor to the view below. This wouldn't be so bad. He wasn't here looking over her shoulder, barking orders. And really, in terms of work space, this office could hardly be beat.

Maybe this job wouldn't be so bad, after all.

By the time Jonathan made a run to town after finishing up with the horses, it was past lunchtime.

So he brought food from the Crab Shanty and hoped his new assistant didn't have a horrible allergy to seafood.

He probably should have checked. He wasn't really used to considering other people. And he couldn't say he was looking forward to getting used to it. But he would rather she didn't die. At least, not while at work.

He held tightly to the white bag of food as he made his way to the office. Her back was to the door, her head bent low over a stack of papers, one hand poised on the mouse.

He set the bag down loudly on the table by the doorway, then deposited his keys there, too. He hung his hat on the hook. "Hungry?"

Her head popped up, her eyes wide. "Oh, I didn't hear you come in. You scared me. You should have announced yourself or something."

"I just did. I said, 'hungry?' I mean, I could have said I'm here, but how is that any different?"

She shook her head. "I don't have an answer to that."

"Great. I have fish."

"What kind?"

"Fried kind."

"I approve."

He sighed in mock relief. "Good. Because if you didn't, I don't know how I would live with myself. I would have had to eat both of these." He opened the bag, taking out two cartons and two cans of Coke.

He sat in the chair in front of the table he used for drawing plans, then held her portion toward her.

She made a funny face, then accepted the offered lunch. "Is one of the Cokes for me, too?"

"Sure," he said, sliding a can at her.

She blinked, then took the can.

"What?"

She shook her head. "Nothing."

"You expected me to hand everything to you, didn't you?"

She shook her head. "No. Well, maybe. But, I'm sorry. I don't work with my father anymore, as you have mentioned more than once."

"No," he said, "you don't. And this isn't a church. Though—" he took a french fry out of the box and bit it "—this is pretty close to a religious experience." He picked up one of the thoughtfully included napkins and wiped his fingers before popping the top on the Coke can.

"How did you know I worked at the church?" she asked.

"I pay attention. And I definitely looked at the address you included on your form. Also, I know your brother. Or rather, I know of him. My sister is engaged to his brother-in-law. I might not be chummy with him, but I know his dad is the pastor. And that he has a younger sister."

She looked crestfallen. "I didn't realize you knew my brother."

"Is that a problem?"

"I was trying to get a job based on my own merit. Not on family connections. And frankly, I can't find anyone who is not connected to my family in some way in this town. My father knows the saints, my brother knows the sinners."

"Are you calling me a sinner?"

She picked gingerly at a piece of fish. "All have sinned and so forth."

"That isn't what you meant."

She suddenly became very interested in her coleslaw, prodding it with her plastic fork.

"How is it you know I'm a sinner?" he asked, not intending to let her off the hook, because this was just so fun. Hell, he'd gone and hired himself a church secretary, so might as well play with her a little bit.

"I didn't mean that," she insisted, her cheeks turning pink. He couldn't remember the last time he'd seen a woman blush.

"Well, if it helps at all, I don't know your brother well. I just buy alcohol from him on the weekends. But you're right. I am a sinner, Hayley."

She looked up at him then. The shock reflected in those stormy eyes touched him down deep. Made his stomach feel tight, made his blood feel hot. All right, he needed to get a handle on himself. Because that was not the kind of fun he was going to have with the church secretary he had hired. No way.

Jonathan Bear was a ruthless bastard; that fact could not be disputed. He had learned to look out for himself at an early age, because no one else would. Not his father. Certainly not his mother, who had taken off when he was a teenager, leaving him with a younger sister to raise. And most definitely not anyone in town.

But, even he had a conscience.

In theory, anyway.

"Good to know. I mean, since we're getting to know each other, I guess."

They ate in relative silence after that. Jonathan took that opportunity to check messages on his phone. A damn smartphone. This was what he had come to. Used to be that if he wanted to spend time alone he could unplug and go out on his horse easily enough. Now, he could still do that, but his business partners—dammit all, he had business partners—knew that he should be accessible and was opting not to be.

"Why did you leave the church?" he asked after a long stretch of silence.

"I didn't. I mean, not as a member. But, I couldn't work there anymore. You know, I woke up one morning and looked in the mirror and imagined doing that exact same thing in forty years. Sitting behind that desk, in the same chair, talking to the same people, having the same conversations… I just didn't think I could do it. I thought…well, for a long time I thought if I sat in that chair life would come to me." She took a deep breath. "But it won't. I have to go get it."

What she was talking about… That kind of stability. It was completely foreign to him. Jonathan could scarcely remember a time in his life when things had stayed the same from year to year. He would say one thing for poverty, it was dynamic. It could be a grind, sure, but it kept you on your toes. He'd constantly looked for new ways to support himself and Rebecca. To prove to child services that he was a fit guardian. To keep their dwelling up to par, to make sure they could always afford it. To keep them both fed and clothed—or at least her, if not him.

He had always craved what Hayley was talking about. A place secure enough to rest for a while. But not having it was why he was here now. In this house, with all this money. Which was the only real damned security in the world. Making sure you were in control of everything around you.

Even if it did mean owning a fucking smartphone.

"So, your big move was to be my assistant?"

She frowned. "No. This is my small move. You have to make small moves before you can make a big one."

That he agreed with, more or less. His whole life had been a series of small moves with no pausing in between. One step at a time as he climbed up to the top. "I'm not sure it's the best thing to let your employer know you think he's a small step," he said, just because he wanted to see her cheeks turn pink again. He was gratified when they did.

"Sorry. This is a giant step for me. I intend to stay here forever in my elevated position as your assistant."

He set his lunch down, leaning back and holding up his hands. "Slow down, baby. I'm not looking for a commitment."

At that, her cheeks turned bright red. She took another bite of coleslaw, leaving a smear of mayonnaise on the corner of her mouth. Without thinking, he leaned in and brushed his thumb across the smudge, and along the edge of her lower lip.

He didn't realize it was a mistake until the slug of heat hit him low and fast in the gut.

He hadn't realized it would be a mistake because she was such a mousy little thing, a church secretary. Because his taste didn't run to that kind of thing. At least, that's what he would have said.

But while his brain might have a conscience, he discovered in that moment that his body certainly did not.

Three

It was like striking a match, his thumb sweeping across her skin. It left a trail of fire where he touched, and made her feel hot in places he hadn't. She was… Well, she was immobilized.

Like a deer caught in the headlights, seeing exactly what was barreling down on her, and unable to move.

Except, of course, Jonathan wasn't barreling down on her. He wasn't moving at all.

He was just looking at her, his dark eyes glittering, his expression like granite. She followed his lead, unsure of what to do. Of how she should react.

And then, suddenly, everything clicked into place. Exactly what she was feeling, exactly what she was doing…and exactly how much of an idiot she was.

She took a deep breath, gasping as though she'd been submerged beneath water. She turned her chair sideways, facing the computer again. "Well," she said, "thank you for lunch."

Fiddlesticks. And darn it. And fudging graham crackers.

She had just openly stared at her boss, probably looking like a guppy gasping on dry land because he had wiped mayonnaise off her lip. Which was— as things went—probably one of the more platonic touches a man and a woman could share.

The problem was, she couldn't remember ever being touched—even platonically—by a man who wasn't family. So she had been completely un-prepared for the reaction it created inside her. Which she had no doubt he'd noticed.

Attraction. She had felt *attracted* to him.

Backtracking, she realized the tight feeling in her stomach that had appeared the first moment she'd seen him was probably attraction.

That was bad. Very bad.

But what she was really curious about, was why this attraction felt different from what she'd felt around other men she had liked. She'd felt fluttery feelings before. Most notably for Grant Daniels, the junior high youth pastor, a couple years ago. She had really liked him, and she was pretty sure he'd liked her, too, but he hadn't seemed willing to make a move.

She had conversations with him over coffee in the Fellowship Hall, where he had brought up his feelings on dating—he didn't—and how he was waiting until he was ready to get married before getting into any kind of relationship with a woman.

For a while, she'd been convinced he'd told her that because he was close to being ready, and he might want to marry her.

Another instance of sitting, waiting and believing what she wanted would come to her through the sheer force of her good behavior.

Looking back, she realized it was kind of stupid that she had hoped he'd marry her. She didn't know him, not really. She had only ever seen him around church, and of course her feelings for him were based on that. Everybody was on their best behavior there. Including her.

Not that she actually behaved badly, which was kind of the problem. There was what she did, what she showed the world, and then there were the dark, secret things that lived inside her. Things she wanted but was afraid to pursue.

The fluttery feelings she had for Grant were like public Hayley. Smiley, shiny and giddy. Wholesome and hopeful.

The tension she felt in her stomach when she looked at Jonathan…that was all secret Hayley.

And it scared her that there was another person who seemed to have access to those feelings she examined only late at night in the darkness of her room.

She had finally gotten up the courage to buy a romance novel when she'd been at the grocery store a month or so ago. She had always been curious about those books, but since she'd lived with her parents, she had never been brave enough to buy one.

So, at the age of twenty-four, she had gotten her very first one. And it had been educational. Very, *very* educational. She had been a little afraid of it, to be honest.

Because those illicit feelings brought about late at night by hazy images and the slide of sheets against her bare skin had suddenly become focused and specific after reading that book.

And if that book had been the fantasy, Jonathan was the reality. It made her want to turn tail and run. But she couldn't. Because if she did, then he would know what no one else knew about her.

She couldn't risk him knowing.

They were practically strangers. They had nothing in common. These feelings were ridiculous. At least Grant had been the kind of person she was suited to.

Which begged the question—why didn't he make her feel this off-kilter?

Her face felt like it was on fire, and she was sure

Jonathan could easily read her reaction. That was the problem. It had taken her longer to understand what she was feeling than it had likely taken him. Because he wasn't sheltered like she was.

Sheltered even from her own desire.

The word made her shiver. Because it was one she had avoided thinking until now.

Desire.

Did she desire him? And if she did, what did that mean?

Her mouth went dry as several possibilities floated through her mind. Each more firmly rooted in fantasy than the last, since she had no practical experience with any of this.

And it was going to stay that way. At least for now.

Small steps. This job was her first small step. And it was a job, not a chance for her to get ridiculous over a man.

"Did you have anything else you wanted me to do?" she asked, not turning to face him, keeping her gaze resolutely pinned to the computer screen.

He was silent for a moment, and for some reason, the silence felt thick. "Did you finish entering the invoices?"

"Yes."

"Good," he said. "Here." He handed her his phone. "If anyone calls, say I'm not available, but you're happy to take a message. And I want you to call the county office and ask about the permits listed in the other spreadsheet I have open. Just get a status update on that. Do you cook?"

She blinked. "What?"

"Do you cook? I hired you to be my assistant. Which includes things around the house. And I eat around the house."

"I cook," she said, reeling from the change of topic.

"Great. Have something ready for me, and if I'm not back before you knock off at five, just keep it warm."

Then he turned and walked out, leaving her feeling both relieved and utterly confused. All those positive thoughts from this morning seemed to be coming back to haunt her, mock her.

The work she could handle. It was the man that scared her.

The first week of working with Hayley had been pretty good, in spite of that hiccup on the first day.

The one where he had touched her skin and felt just how soft it was. Something he never should have done.

But she was a good assistant. And every evening when he came in from dealing with ranch work his dinner was ready. That had been kind of a dick move, asking her to cook, but in truth, he hadn't put a very detailed job description in the ad. And she wasn't an employee of Gray Bear. She was his personal employee, and that meant he could expand her responsibilities.

At least, that was what he told himself as he approached the front porch Friday evening, his stomach already growling in anticipation. When he came in for the evening after the outside work was done, she was usually gone and the food was warming in the oven.

It was like having a wife. With none of the drawbacks *and* none of the perks.

But considering he could get those perks from a woman who wasn't in his house more than forty hours a week, he would take this happily.

He stomped up the front steps, kicking his boots off before he went inside. He'd been walking through sludge in one of the far pastures and he didn't want to track in mud. His housekeeper didn't come until later in the week.

The corner of his mouth lifted as he processed that thought. He had a housekeeper. He didn't have to get on his hands and knees and scrub floors anymore. Which he had done. More times than he would care to recount. Most of the time the house he and Rebecca had shared while growing up had been messy.

It was small, and their belongings—basic though they were—created a lot of clutter. Plus, teenage boys weren't the best at keeping things deep cleaned. Especially not when they also had full-time jobs and were trying to finish high school. But when he knew child services would be by, he did his best.

He didn't now. He paid somebody else to do it. For a long time, adding those kinds of expenses had made both pride and anxiety burn in his gut. Adjusting to living at a new income level was not seamless. And since things had grown exponentially and so quickly, the adjustments had come even harder. Often in a million ways he couldn't anticipate. But he was working on it. Hiring a housekeeper. Hiring Hayley.

Pretty soon, he would give in and buy himself a new pair of boots.

He drew nearer to the kitchen, smelling something good. And then he heard footsteps, the clattering of dishes.

He braced his arms on either side of the doorway. Clearly, she hadn't heard him approach. She was bending down to pull something out of the oven, her sweet ass outlined to perfection by that prim little skirt.

There was absolutely nothing provocative about it. It fell down past her knees, and when she stood straight it didn't display any curves whatsoever.

For a moment, he just admired his own commitment to being a dick. She could not be dressed more appropriately, and still his eyes were glued to her butt. And damn, his body liked what he saw.

"You're still here," he said, pushing away from

the door and walking into the room. He had to break the tension stretching tight inside him. Step one was breaking the silence and making his presence known. Step two was going to be calling up one of the women he had associations with off and on.

Because he had to do something to take the edge off. Clearly, it had been too long since he'd gotten laid.

"Sorry," she said, wiping her hands on a dishcloth and making a few frantic movements. As though she wanted to look industrious, but didn't exactly have a specific task. "The roast took longer than I thought it would. But I did a little more paperwork while I waited. And I called the county to track down that permit."

"You don't have to justify all your time. Everything has gotten done this week. Plus, inefficient meat preparation was not on my list of reasons I might fire you."

She shrugged. "I thought you reserved the right to revise that list at any time."

"I do. But not today."

"I should be out of your hair soon." She walked around the counter and he saw she was barefoot. Earlier, he had been far too distracted by her backside to notice.

"Pretty sure that's a health code violation," he said.

She turned pink all the way up to her scalp. "Sorry. My feet hurt."

He thought of those low, sensible heels she always

wore and he had to wonder what the point was to wearing shoes that ugly if they weren't even comfortable. The kind of women he usually went out with wore the kinds of shoes made for sitting. Or dancing on a pole.

But Hayley didn't look like she even knew what pole dancing was, let alone like she would jump up there and give it a try. She was... Well, she was damn near sweet.

Which was all wrong for him, in every way. He wasn't sweet.

He was successful. He was driven.

But he was temporary at best. And frankly, almost everyone in his life seemed grateful for that fact. No one stayed. Not his mother, not his father. Even his sister was off living her own life now.

So why he should spend even one moment looking at Hayley the way he'd been looking at her, he didn't know. He didn't have time for subtlety. He never had. He had always liked obvious women. Women who asked for what they wanted without any game-playing or shame.

He didn't want a wife. He didn't even want a serious girlfriend. Hell, he didn't want a casual girlfriend. When he went out it was with the express intention of hooking up. When it came to women, he didn't like a challenge.

His whole damned life was a challenge, and always had been. When he'd been raising his sister he couldn't bring anyone back to his place, which meant he needed someone with a place of their own, or someone willing to get busy in the back of a pickup truck.

Someone who understood he had only a couple free hours, and he wouldn't be sharing their bed all night.

Basically, his taste ran toward women who were all the things Hayley wasn't.

Cute ass or not.

None of those thoughts did anything to ease the tension in his stomach. No matter how succinctly they broke down just why he shouldn't find Hayley hot.

He nearly scoffed. She *wasn't* hot. She was… She would not be out of place as the wholesome face on a baking mix. Much more Little Debbie than Debbie Does Dallas.

"It's fine. I don't want you going lame on me."

She grinned. "No. Then you'd have to put me down."

"True. And if I lose more than one personal assistant that way people will start asking questions."

He could tell she wasn't sure if he was kidding or not. For a second, she looked downright concerned.

"I have not sent, nor do I intend to send, any of my employees—present or former—to the glue factory. Don't look at me like that."

She bit her lower lip, and that forced him to spend

a moment examining just how lush it was. He didn't like that. She needed to stop bending over, and to do nothing that would draw attention to her mouth. Maybe, when he revised the list of things he might fire her for, he would add drawing attention to attractive body parts to the list.

"I can never tell when you're joking."

"Me, either," he said.

That time she did laugh. "You know," she said, "you could smile."

"Takes too much energy."

The timer went off and she bustled back to the stove. "Okay," she said, "it should be ready now." She pulled a little pan out of the oven and took the lid off. It was full of roast and potatoes, carrots and onions. The kind of home-cooked meal he imagined a lot of kids grew up on.

For him, traditional fare had been more along the lines of flour tortillas with cheese or ramen noodles. Something cheap, easy and full of carbs. Just enough to keep you going.

His stomach growled in appreciation, and that was the kind of hunger associated with Hayley that he could accept.

"I should go," she said, starting to walk toward the kitchen door.

"Stay."

As soon as he made the offer Jonathan wanted to bite his tongue off. He did not need to encourage spending more time in closed off spaces with her. Although dinner might be a good chance to prove that he could easily master those weird bursts of attraction.

"No," she said, and he found himself strangely relieved. "I should go."

"Don't be an idiot," he said, surprising himself yet again. "Dinner is ready here. And it's late. Plus there's no way I can eat all this."

"Okay," she said, clearly hesitant.

"Come on now. Stop looking at me like you think I'm going to bite you. You've been reading too much *Twilight*. Indians don't really turn into wolves."

Her face turned really red then. "That's not what I was thinking. I don't... I'm not afraid of you."

She was afraid of something. And what concerned him most was that it might be the same thing he was fighting against.

"I really was teasing you," he said. "I have a little bit of a reputation in town, but I didn't earn half of it."

"Are you saying people in town are...prejudiced?"

"I wouldn't go that far. I mean, I wouldn't say it's on purpose. But whether it's because I grew up poor or it's because I'm brown, people have always given me a wide berth."

"I didn't... I mean, I've never seen people act that way."

"Well, they wouldn't. Not to you."

She blinked slightly. "I'll serve dinner now."

"Don't worry," he said, "the story has a happy ending. I have a lot of money now, and that trumps anything else. People have no issue hiring me to build these days. Though, I remember the first time my old boss put me on as the leader of the building crew, and the guy whose house we were building had a problem with it. He didn't think I should be doing anything that required too much skill. Was more comfortable with me just swinging the hammer, not telling other people where to swing it."

She took plates down from the cupboard, holding them close to her chest. "That's awful."

"People are awful."

A line creased her forehead. "They definitely can be."

"Stop hugging my dinner plate to your shirt. That really isn't sanitary. We can eat in here." He gestured to the countertop island. She set the plates down hurriedly, then started dishing food onto them.

He sighed heavily, moving to where she was and taking the big fork and knife out of her hands. "Have a seat. How much do you want?"

"Oh," she said, "I don't need much."

He ignored her, filling the plate completely, then filling his own. After that, he went to the fridge and pulled out a beer. "Want one?"

She shook her head. "I don't drink."

He frowned, then looked back into the fridge. "I don't have anything else."

"Water is fine."

He got her a glass and poured some water from the spigot in the fridge. He handed it to her, regarding her like she was some kind of alien life-form. The small conversation had really highlighted the gulf between them.

It should make him feel even more ashamed about looking at her butt.

Except shame was pretty hard for him to come by.

"Tell me what you think about people, Hayley." He took a bite of the roast and nearly gave her a raise then and there.

"No matter what things look like on the surface, you never know what someone is going through. It surprised me how often someone who had been smiling on Sunday would come into the office and break down in tears on Tuesday afternoon, saying they needed to talk to the pastor. Everyone has problems, and I do my best not to add to them."

"That's a hell of a lot nicer than most people deserve."

"Okay, what do you think about people?" she asked, clasping her hands in front of her and looking so damn interested and sincere he wasn't quite sure how to react.

"I think they're a bunch of self-interested bastards. And that's fair enough, because so am I. But whenever somebody asks for something, or offers me something, I ask myself what they will get out of it. If I can't figure out how they'll benefit, that's when I get worried."

"Not everyone is after money or power," she said. He could see she really believed what she said. He wasn't sure what to make of that.

"All right," he conceded, "maybe they aren't all after money. But they are looking to gain something. Everyone is. You can't get through life any other way. Trust me."

"I don't know. I never thought of it that way. In terms of who could get me what. At least, that's not how I've lived."

"Then you're an anomaly."

She shook her head. "My father is like that, too. He really does want to help people. He cares. Pastoring a small church in a little town doesn't net you much power or money."

"Of course it does. You hold the power of people's salvation in your hands. Pass around the plate every week. Of course you get power and money." Jonathan shook his head. "Being the leader of local spirituality is power, honey, trust me."

Her cheeks turned pink. "Okay. You might have a point. But my father doesn't claim to have the key to anyone's salvation. And the money in that basket goes right back into the community. Or into keeping the doors of the church open. My father believes in living the same way the community lives. Not higher up. So whatever baggage you might have about church, that's specific to your experience. It has nothing to do with my father or his faith."

She spoke with such raw certainty that Jonathan was tempted to believe her. But he knew too much about human nature.

Still, he liked all that conviction burning inside her. He liked that she believed what she said, even if he couldn't.

If he had been born with any ideals, he couldn't remember them now. He'd never had the luxury of having faith in humanity, as Hayley seemed to have. No, his earliest memory of his father was the old man's fist connecting with his face. Jonathan had never had the chance to believe the best of anybody.

He had been introduced to the worst far too early.

And he didn't know very many people who'd had different experiences.

The optimism she seemed to carry, the softness combined with strength, fascinated him. He wanted to draw closer to it, to her, to touch her skin, to see if she was strong enough to take the physical demands he put on a woman who shared his bed.

To see how shocked she might be when he told her what those demands were. In explicit detail.

He clenched his jaw tight, clamping his teeth down hard. He was not going to find out, for a couple reasons. The first being that she was his employee, and off-limits. The second being that all those things that fascinated him would be destroyed if he got close, if he laid even one finger on her.

Cynicism bled from his pores, and he damn well knew it. He had earned it. He wasn't one of those bored rich people overcome by ennui just because life had gone so well he wanted to create problems so he had something to battle against.

No. He had fought every step of the way, and he had been disappointed by people in every way imaginable. He had earned his feelings about people, that was for damn sure.

But he wasn't certain he wanted to pass that cynicism on to Hayley. No, she was like a pristine wilderness area. Unspoiled by humans. And his first inclination was to explore every last inch, to experience all that beauty, all that majesty. But he had to leave it alone. He had to leave it looked at, not touched.

Hayley Thompson was the same. Untouched. He had to leave her unspoiled. Exploring that beauty would only leave it ruined, and he couldn't do that. He wouldn't.

"I think it's sad," she said, her voice muted. "That you can't see the good in other people."

"I've been bitten in the ass too many times," he said, his tone harder than he'd intended it to be. "I'm glad you haven't been."

"I haven't had the chance to be. But that's kind

of the point of what I'm doing. Going out, maybe getting bitten in the ass." Her cheeks turned bright red. "I can't believe I said that."

"What?"

"That word."

That made his stomach feel like it had been hollowed out. *"Ass?"*

Her cheeks turned even redder. "Yes. I don't say things like that."

"I guess not… Being the church secretary and all."

Now he just felt… Well, she made him feel rough and uncultured, dirty and hard and unbending as steel. Everything she was not. She was small, delicate and probably far too easy to break. Just like he'd imagined earlier, she was…set apart. Unspoiled. And here he had already spoiled her a little bit. She'd said ass, right there in his kitchen.

And she'd looked shocked as hell by her own behavior.

"You don't have to say things like that if you don't want to," he said. "Not every experience is a good experience. You shouldn't try things just to try them. Hell, if I'd had the choice of staying innocent of human nature, maybe I would have taken that route instead. Don't ruin that nice vision of the world you have."

She frowned. "You know, everybody talks about going out and experiencing things…"

"Sure. But when people say that, they want control over those experiences. Believe me, having the blinders ripped off is not necessarily the best thing."

She nodded slowly. "I guess I understand that. What kinds of experiences do you think are bad?"

Immediately, he thought of about a hundred bad things he wanted to do to her. Most of them in bed, all of them naked. He sucked in a sharp breath through his teeth. "I don't think we need to get into that."

"I'm curious."

"You know what they say about curiosity and the cat, right?"

"But I'm not a cat."

"No," he said, "you are Hayley, and you should be grateful for the things you've been spared. Maybe you should even go back to the church office."

"No," she said, frowning. "I don't want to. Maybe I don't want to *experience everything*—I can see how you're probably right about that. But I can't just stay in one place, sheltered for the rest of my life. I have to figure out…who I am and what I want."

That made him laugh, because it was such a naive sentiment. He had never stood back and asked himself who the hell Jonathan Bear was, and what he wanted out of life. He hadn't given a damn how he made his money as long as he made it.

As far as he was concerned, dreams were for people with a lot of time on their hands. He had to *do*. Even as a kid, he couldn't think, couldn't wonder; he had to act.

She might as well be speaking a foreign language. "You'll have to tell me what that's like."

"What?"

"That quest to find yourself. Let me know if it's any more effective than just living your life and seeing what happens."

"Okay, now you've made me feel silly."

He took another bite of dinner. Maybe he should back down, because he didn't want her to quit. He would like to continue eating her food. And, frankly, he would like to keep looking at her.

Just because he should back down didn't mean he was going to.

"There was no safety net in my life," he said, not bothering to reassure her. "There never has been. I had to work my ass off from the moment I was old enough to get paid to do something. Hell, even before then. I would get what I could from the store, expired products, whatever, so we would have something to eat. That teaches you a lot about yourself. You don't have to go looking. In those situations, you find out whether you're a survivor or not. Turns out I am. And I've never really seen what more I needed to know."

"I don't… I don't have anything to say to that."

"Yeah," he returned. "My life story is kind of a bummer."

"Not now," she said softly. "You have all this. You have the business, you have this house."

"Yeah, I expect a man could find himself here. Well, unless he got lost because it was so big." He smiled at her, but she didn't look at all disarmed by the gesture. Instead, she looked thoughtful, and that made his stomach feel tight.

He didn't really do meaningful conversation. He especially didn't do it with women.

Yet here he was, telling this woman more about himself than he could remember telling anyone. Rebecca knew everything, of course. Well, as much as she'd observed while being a kid in that situation. They didn't need to talk about it. It was just life. But other people... Well, he didn't see the point in talking about the deficit he'd started with. He preferred people assume he'd sprung out of the ground powerful and successful. They took him more seriously.

He'd had enough disadvantages, and he wouldn't set himself up for any more.

But there was something about Hayley—her openness, her honesty—that made him want to talk. That made him feel bad for being insincere. Because she was just so...so damn real.

How would he have been if he'd had a softer existence? Maybe he wouldn't be as hard. Maybe a different life would have meant not breaking a woman like this the moment he put his hands on her.

It was moot. Because he hadn't had a different

life. And if he had, he probably wouldn't have made half as much of himself.

"You don't have to feel bad for wanting more," he said finally. "Just because other people don't have it easy, doesn't mean you don't have your own kind of hard."

"It's just difficult to decide what to do when other people's expectations feel so much bigger than your own dreams."

"I know a little something about that. Only in my case, the expectations other people had for me were that I would end up dead of a drug overdose or in prison. So, all things considered, I figured I would blow past those expectations and give people something to talk about."

"I just want to travel."

"Is that it?"

A smile played in the corner of her lips, and he found himself wondering what it might be like to taste that smile. "Okay. And see a famous landmark. Like the Eiffel Tower or Big Ben. And I want to dance."

"Have you never danced?"

"No!" She looked almost comically horrified. "Where would I have danced?"

"Well, your brother does own a bar. And there is line dancing."

"I can't even go into Ace's bar. My parents don't go. We can go to the brewery. Because they serve more food there. And it's not called a bar."

"That seems like some arbitrary shit."

Her cheeks colored, and he didn't know if it was because he'd pointed out a flaw in her parents' logic or because he had cursed. "Maybe. But I follow their lead. It's important for us to keep away from the appearance of evil."

"Now, that I don't know anything about. Because nobody cares much about my appearance."

She cleared her throat. "So," she said. "Dancing."

Suddenly, an impulse stole over him, one he couldn't quite understand or control. Before he knew it, he was pushing his chair back and standing up, extending his hand. "All right, Hayley Thompson, Paris has to wait awhile. But we can take care of the dancing right now."

"What?" Her pretty eyes flew wide, her soft lips rounded into a perfect O.

"Dance with me, Hayley."

Four

Hayley was pretty sure she was hallucinating.

Because there was no way her stern boss was standing there, his large, work-worn hand stretched toward her, his dark eyes glittering with an intensity she could only guess at the meaning of, having just asked her to dance. Except, no matter how many times she blinked, he was still standing there. And the words were still echoing in her head.

"There's no music."

He took his cell phone out of his pocket, opened an app and set the phone on the table, a slow country song filling the air. "There," he said. "Music accomplished. Now, dance with me."

"I thought men *asked* for a dance, I didn't think they demanded one."

"Some men, maybe. But not me. But remember, I don't give a damn about appearances."

"I think I might admire that about you."

"You should," he said, his tone grave.

She felt... Well, she felt breathless and fluttery, and she didn't know what to do. But if she said no, then he would know just how inexperienced she was. He would know she was making a giant internal deal about his hand touching hers, about the possibility of being held against his body. That she felt strange, unnerving sensations skittering over her skin when she looked at him. She was afraid he could see her too clearly.

Isn't this what you wanted? To reach out? To take a chance?

It was. So she did.

She took his hand. She was still acclimating to his heat, to being touched by him, skin to skin, when she found herself pressed flush against his chest, his hand enveloping hers. He wrapped his arm around her waist, his palm hot on her lower back.

She shivered. She didn't know why. Because she wasn't cold. No. She was hot. And so was he. Hot and hard, so much harder than she had imagined another person could be.

She had never, ever been this close to a man before. Had never felt a man's skin against hers. His hand was rough, from all that hard work. What might it feel like if he touched her skin elsewhere? If he pushed his other hand beneath her shirt and slid his fingertips against her lower back?

That thought sent a sharp pang straight to her stomach, unfurling something inside her, making her blood run faster.

She stared straight at his shoulder, at an innocuous spot on his flannel shirt. Because she couldn't bring herself to raise her eyes and look at that hard, lean face, at the raw beauty she had never fully appreciated before.

He would probably be offended to be characterized as beautiful. But he was. In the same way that a mountain was beautiful. Tall, strong and unmoving.

She gingerly curled her fingers around his shoulder, while he took the lead, his hold on her firm and sure as he established a rhythm she could follow.

The grace in his steps surprised her. Caused her to meet his gaze. She both regretted it and relished it at the same time. Because it was a shame to stare at flannel when she could be looking into those dark eyes, but they also made her feel…absolutely and completely undone.

"Where did you learn to dance?" she asked, her voice sounding as breathless as she had feared it might.

But she was curious about this man who had grown up in such harsh circumstances, who had clearly devoted most of his life to hard work with no frills, who had learned to do this.

"A woman," he said, a small smile tugging at the edges of his lips.

She was shocked by the sudden, sour turn in her stomach. It was deeply unpleasant, and she didn't know what to do to make it stop. Imagining what other woman he might have learned this from, how he might have held her…

It hurt. In the strangest way.

"Was she…somebody special to you? Did you love her?"

His smile widened. "No. I've never loved anybody. Not anybody besides my sister. But I sure as hell *wanted* something from that woman, and she wanted to dance."

It took Hayley a while to figure out the meaning behind those words. "Oh," she said, "she wanted to dance and you wanted…" That feeling in her stomach intensified, but along with it came a strange sort of heat. Because he was holding *her* now, dancing with her. *She* wanted to dance. Did that mean that he…?

"Don't look at me like that, Hayley. This," he said, tightening his hold on her and dipping her slightly, his face moving closer to hers, "is just a dance."

She was a tangle of unidentified feelings—knots in her stomach, an ache between her thighs—and she didn't want to figure out what any of it meant.

"Good," she said, wishing she could have infused some conviction into that word.

The music slowed, the bass got heavier. And he matched the song effortlessly, his hips moving firmly against hers with every deep pulse of the beat.

This time, she couldn't ignore the lyrics. About two people and the fire they created together. She wouldn't have fully understood what that meant even a few minutes ago, but in Jonathan's arms, with the heat that burned from his body, fire was what she felt.

Like her nerve endings had been set ablaze, like a spark had been stoked low inside her. If he moved in just the wrong way—or just the right way—the flames in him would catch hold of that spark in her and they would combust.

She let her eyes flutter closed, gave herself over to the moment, to the song, to the feel of him, the scent of him. She was dancing. And she liked it a lot more than she had anticipated and in a way she hadn't imagined she could.

She had pictured laughing, lightness, with people all around, like at the bar she had never been to before. But this was something else. A deep intimacy that grew from somewhere inside her chest and intensified as the music seemed to draw them more tightly together.

She drew in a breath, letting her eyes open and look up at him. And then she froze.

He was staring at her, the glitter in his dark eyes

almost predatory. She didn't know why that word came to mind. Didn't even know what it might mean in this context. When a man looked at you like he was a wildcat and you were a potential meal.

Then her eyes dipped down to his mouth. Her own lips tingled in response and she was suddenly aware of how dry they were. She slid her tongue over them, completely self-conscious about the action even as she did it, yet unable to stop.

She was satisfied when that predatory light in his eyes turned sharper. More intense.

She didn't know what she was doing. But she found herself moving closer to him. She didn't know why. She just knew she had to. With the same bone-deep impulse that came with the need to draw breath, she had to lean in closer to Jonathan Bear. She couldn't fight it; she didn't want to. And until her lips touched his, she didn't even know what she was moving toward.

But when their mouths met, it all became blindingly clear.

She had thought about these feelings in terms of fire, but this sensation was something bigger, something infinitely more destructive. This was an explosion. One she felt all the way down to her toes; one that hit every place in between.

She was shaking. Trembling like a leaf in the wind. Or maybe even like a tree in a storm.

He was the storm.

His hold changed. He let go of her hand, withdrew his arm from around her waist, pressed both palms against her cheeks as he took the kiss deeper, harder.

It was like drowning. Like dying. Only she didn't want to fight it. Didn't want to turn away. She couldn't have, even if she'd tried. Because his grip was like iron, his body like a rock wall. They weren't moving in time with the music anymore. No. This was a different rhythm entirely. He propelled her backward, until her shoulder blades met with the dining room wall, his hard body pressed against hers.

He was hard. Everywhere. Hard chest, hard stomach, hard thighs. And that insistent hardness pressing against her hip.

She gasped when she realized what that was. And he consumed her shocked sound, taking advantage of her parted lips to slide his tongue between them.

She released her hold on him, her hands floating up without a place to land, and she curled her fingers into fists. She surrendered herself to the kiss, to him. His hold was tight enough to keep her anchored to the earth, to keep her anchored to him.

She let him have control. Let him take the lead. She didn't know how to dance, and she didn't know how to do this. But he did.

So she let him show her. This was on her list, too, though she hadn't been brave enough to say it, even to herself. To know passion. To experience her first kiss.

She wanted it to go on and on. She never wanted it to end. If she could just be like this, those hot hands cupping her face, that insistent mouth devouring hers, she was pretty sure she could skip the Eiffel Tower.

She felt him everywhere, not just his kiss, not just his touch. Her breasts felt heavy. They ached. In any other circumstances, she might be horrified by that. But she didn't possess the capacity to be horrified, not right now. Not when everything else felt so good. She wasn't ashamed; she wasn't embarrassed—not of the heavy feeling in her breasts, not of the honeyed, slick feeling between her thighs.

This just made sense.

Right now, what she felt was the only thing that made sense. It was the only thing she wanted.

Kissing Jonathan Bear was a necessity.

He growled, flexing his hips toward hers, making it so she couldn't ignore his arousal. And the evidence of his desire carved out a hollow feeling inside her. Made her shake, made her feel like her knees had dissolved into nothing and that without his powerful hold she would crumple onto the floor.

She still wasn't touching him. Her hands were still away from his body, trembling. But she didn't want to do anything to break the moment. Didn't want to make a sound, didn't want to make the wrong move. She didn't want to turn him off or scare him away.

Didn't want to do anything to telegraph her innocence. Because it would probably freak him out.

*Right, Hayley, like he totally believes you're a sex
kitten who's kissed a hundred men.*

She didn't know what to do with her hands, let
alone her lips, her tongue. She was receiving, not
giving. But she had a feeling if she did anything else
she would look like an idiot.

Suddenly, he released his hold on her, moving
away from her so quickly she might have thought
she'd hurt him.

She was dazed, still leaning against the wall.
If she hadn't been, she would have collapsed. Her
hands were still in the air, clenched into fists, and
her breath came in short, harsh bursts. So did his,
if the sharp rise and fall of his chest was anything
to go by.

"That was a mistake," he said, his voice hard. His
words were everything she had feared they might be.

"No, it wasn't," she said, her lips feeling numb,
and a little bit full, making it difficult for her to talk.
Or maybe the real difficulty came from feeling like
her head was filled with bees, buzzing all around
and scrambling her thoughts.

"Yes," he said, his voice harder, "it was."

"No," she insisted. "It was a great kiss. A really,
really good kiss. I didn't want it to end."

Immediately, she regretted saying that. Because
it had been way too revealing. She supposed it was

incredibly gauche to tell the guy you'd just kissed that you could have kissed him forever. She tried to imagine how Grant, the youth pastor, might have reacted to that. He would have told her she needed to go to an extra Bible study. Or that she needed to marry him first.

He certainly wouldn't have looked at her the way Jonathan was. Like he wanted to eat her whole, but was barely restraining himself from doing just that. "That's exactly the problem," he returned, the words like iron, "because I *did* want it to end. But in a much different way than it did."

"I don't understand." Her face was hot, and she was humiliated now. So she didn't see why she shouldn't go whole hog. Let him know she was fully outside her comfort zone and she wasn't keeping up with all his implications. She needed stated facts, not innuendo.

"I didn't want to keep kissing you forever. I wanted to pull your top off, shove your skirt up and bury myself inside of you. Is that descriptive enough for you?"

It was. And he had succeeded in shocking her. She wasn't stupid. She knew he was hard, and she knew what that meant. But even given that fact, she hadn't really imagined he wanted... Not with her.

And this was just her first kiss. She wasn't ready for more. Wasn't ready for another step away from the person she had been taught to be.

What about the person you want to be?

She looked at her boss, who was also the most beautiful man she had ever seen. That hadn't been her immediate thought when she'd met him, but she had settled into it as the truth. As certain as the fact the sky was blue and the pine trees that dotted the mountains were deep forest green.

So maybe… Even though it was shocking. Even though it would be a big step, and undoubtedly a big mistake… Maybe she did want it.

"You better go," he said, his voice rough.

"Maybe I don't—"

"You do," he said. "Trust me. And I want you to."

She was confused. Because he had just said he wanted her, and now he was saying he wanted her to go. She didn't understand men. She didn't understand this. She wanted to cry. But a lick of pride slid its way up her spine, keeping her straight, keeping her tears from falling.

Pride she hadn't known she possessed. But then, she hadn't realized she possessed the level of passion that had just exploded between them, either. So it was a day for new discoveries.

"That's fine. I just wanted to have some fun. I can go have it with someone else."

She turned on her heel and walked out of the dining room, out the front door and down the porch steps as quickly as possible. It was dark now, trees like inky bottle brushes rising around her, framing the midnight-blue sky dotted with stars. It was beautiful, but she didn't care. Not right now. She felt... hurt. Emotionally. Physically. The unsatisfied ache between her thighs intensified with the pain growing in her heart.

It was awful. All of it.

It made her want to run. Run back to her parents' house. Run back to the church office.

Being *good* had always been safe.

She had been so certain she wanted to escape safety. Only a few moments earlier she'd needed that escape, felt it might be her salvation. Except she could see now that it was ruin. Utter and complete ruin.

With shaking hands, she pushed the button that undid the locks on her car door and got inside, jamming the key into the ignition and starting it up, a tear sliding down her cheek as she started to back out of the driveway.

She refused to let this ruin her, or this job, or this step she was taking on her own.

She was finding independence, learning new things.

As she turned onto the two-lane highway that would take her back home, she clung to that truth. To the fact that, even though her first kiss had ended somewhat disastrously, it had still shown her something about herself.

It had shown her exactly why it was a good thing she hadn't gotten married to that youthful crush of hers. It would have been dishonest, and not fair to him or to her.

She drove on autopilot, eventually pulling into her driveway and stumbling inside her apartment, lying down on her bed without changing out of her work clothes.

Was she a fallen woman? To want Jonathan like she had. A man she wasn't in love with, a man she wasn't planning to marry.

Had that passion always been there? Or was it created by Jonathan? This feeling. This *need*.

She bit back a sob and forced a smile. She'd had her first kiss. And she wouldn't dwell on what it might mean. Or on the fact that he had sent her away. Or on the fact that—for a moment at least—she had been consumed with the desire for more.

She'd had her first kiss. At twenty-four. And that felt like a change deep inside her body.

Hayley Thompson had a new apartment, a new job, and she had been kissed.

So maybe it wasn't safe. But she had decided she wanted something more than safety, hadn't she?

She would focus on the victories and simply ignore the rest.

No matter that this victory made her body burn in a way that kept her up for the rest of the night.

Five

He hadn't expected her to show up Monday morning. But there she was, in the entryway of the house, hands clasped in front of her, dark hair pulled back in a neat bun. Like she was compensating for what had happened between them Friday night.

"Good morning," he said, taking a sip of his coffee. "I half expected you to take the day off."

"No," she said, her voice shot through with steel, "I can't just take days off. My boss is a tyrant. He'll fire me."

He laughed, mostly to disguise the physical response those words created in him. There was something about her. About all that softness, that innocence, combined with the determination he hadn't realized existed inside her until this moment.

She wasn't just soft, or innocent. She was a force to be reckoned with, and she was bent on showing him that now.

"If he's so bad why do you want to keep the job?"

"My job history is pathetic," she said, walking ahead of him to the stairs. "And, as he has pointed out to me many times, he is not my daddy. My previous boss was. I need something a bit more impressive on my résumé."

"Right. For when you do your traveling."

"Maybe I'll get a job in London," she shot back.

"What's the biggest city you've been to, Hayley?" he asked, following her up the stairs and down the hall toward the office.

"Portland," she said.

He laughed. "London is a little bit bigger."

"I don't care. That's what I want. I want a city where I can walk down the street and not run into anybody that I've ever seen before. All new people. All new faces. I can't imagine that. I can't imagine living a life where I do what I want and not hear a retelling of the night before coming out of my mother's mouth at breakfast the next morning."

"Have you ever done anything worthy of being recounted by your mother?"

Color infused her cheeks. "Okay, specifically, the incident I'm referring to is somebody telling my mother they were proud of me because they saw me giving a homeless woman a dollar."

He laughed. He couldn't help himself, and her cheeks turned an even more intense shade of pink that he knew meant she was furious.

She stamped. Honest to God stamped, like an old-time movie heroine. "What's so funny?"

"Even the gossip about you is good, Hayley Thompson. For the life of me, I can't figure out why you hate that so much."

"Because I can't *do* anything. Jonathan, if you had kissed me in my brother's bar... Can you even imagine? My parents' phone would have been ringing off the hook."

His body hardened at the mention of the kiss. He had been convinced she would avoid the topic.

But he should've known by now that when it came to Hayley he couldn't anticipate her next move. She was more direct, more up-front than he had thought she might be. Was it because of her innocence that she faced things so squarely? Because she hadn't experienced a whole range of consequences for much of anything yet?

"I wouldn't do that to you," he said. "Because you're right. If anybody suspected something unprofessional had happened between us, it would cause trouble for you."

"I didn't mean it that way." She looked horrified.

"I mean, the way people would react if they thought I was… It has nothing to do with you."

"It does. More than you realize. You've been sheltered. But just because you don't know my reputation, that doesn't mean other people in town don't know it. Most people who know you're a good girl know I am a bad man, Hayley. And if anyone suspected I had put my hands on you, I'm pretty sure there would be torches and pitchforks at my front door by sunset."

"Well," she said, "that isn't fair. Because *I* kissed *you*."

"I'm going out on a limb here—of the two of us, I have more experience."

She clasped her hands in front of her and shuffled her feet. "Maybe."

"Maybe nothing, honey. I'm not the kind of man you need to be seen with. So, you're right. You do need to get away. Maybe you should go to London. Hell, I don't know."

"Now you want to get rid of me?"

"Now you're just making it so I can't win."

"I don't mean to," she said, with that trademark sincerity that was no less alarming for being typical of her. "But I don't know what to do with…with this."

She bit her lip, and the motion drew his eye to that lush mouth of hers. Forced him back to the memory of kissing it. Of tasting her.

He wanted her. No question about it.

He couldn't pretend otherwise. But he could at least be honest with himself about why. He wanted her for all the wrong reasons. He wanted her because some sick, caveman part of him wanted to get all that *pretty* dirty. Part of him wanted to corrupt her. To show her everything she was missing. To make her fall from grace a lasting one.

And that was some fucked up shit.

Didn't mean he didn't feel it.

"Well, after I earn enough money, that's probably what I'll do," she said. "And since this isn't going anywhere… I should probably just get to work. And we shouldn't talk about it anymore."

"No," he said, "we shouldn't."

"It was just a kiss."

His stomach twisted. Not because it disappointed him to hear her say that, but because she had to say it for her own peace of mind. She was innocent enough that a kiss worked her up. It meant something to her. Hell, sex barely meant anything to him. Much less a kiss.

Except for hers. You remember hers far too well.

"Just a kiss," he confirmed.

"Good. So give me some spreadsheets."

The rest of the week went well. If well meant dodging moments alone with Jonathan, catching herself staring at him at odd times during the day and having difficulty dreaming of anything except him at night.

"Thank God it's Friday," she said into the emptiness of her living room.

She didn't feel like cooking. She had already made a meal for Jonathan at his house, and then hightailed it out of there as quickly as possible. She knew that if she'd made enough for herself and took food with her he wouldn't have minded, but she was doing her best to keep the lines between them firm.

She couldn't have any more blurred lines. They couldn't have any more…kissing and other weirdness. Just thinking about kissing Jonathan made her feel restless, edgy. She didn't like it. Or maybe she liked it too much.

She huffed out a growl and wandered into the kitchen, opening the cupboard and pulling out a box of chocolate cereal.

It was the kind of cereal her parents never would have bought. Because it wasn't good for you, and it was expensive. So she had bought it for herself, because she had her own job, she was an adult and she made her own decisions.

Do you?

She shut out that snotty little voice. Yes, she *did* make her own decisions. Here she was, living in her own place, working at the job she had chosen. Yes, she very much made her own decisions. She had even kissed Jonathan. Yes, that had been her idea.

Which made the fallout her fault. But she wasn't going to dwell on that.

"I'm dwelling," she muttered. "I'm a liar, and I'm dwelling." She took down a bowl and poured herself a large portion of the chocolaty cereal. Then she stared at it. She didn't want to eat cereal by herself for dinner.

She was feeling restless, reckless.

She was feeling something a whole lot like desperation.

Because of that kiss.

The kiss she had just proposed she wasn't going to think about, the kiss she couldn't let go of. The kiss that made her burn, made her ache and made her wonder about all the mysteries in life she had yet to uncover.

Yeah, *that* kiss.

She had opened a floodgate. She'd uncovered all this potential for passion inside herself, and then she had to stuff it back down deep.

Jonathan Bear was not the only man in the world. Jonathan Bear wasn't even the only man in Copper Ridge.

She could find another guy if she wanted to.

Of course, if she went out, there would be all those gossip issues she and Jonathan had discussed earlier in the week.

That was why she had to get out of this town.

It struck her then, like a horse kicking her square

in the chest, that she was running away. So she could be who she wanted to be without anybody knowing about it. So she could make mistakes and minimize the consequences.

So she could be brave and a coward all at the same time.

That's what it was. It was cowardice. And she was not very impressed with herself.

"Look at you," she scolded, "eating cold cereal on a Friday night by yourself when you would rather be out getting kissed."

Her heart started to beat faster. Where would she go?

And then it hit her. There was one place she could go on a Friday night where nobody from church would recognize her, and even if they did recognize her, they probably wouldn't tell on her because by doing so they would be telling on themselves.

Of course, going there would introduce the problem of her older brother. But Ace had struck out on his own when he was only seventeen years old. He was her inspiration in all this. So he should understand Hayley's need for independence.

And that was when she made her decision. It was Friday night, and she was going out.

She was going to one of the few places in town where she had never set foot before.

Ace's bar.

Six

"I'd like a hamburger," Hayley said, adjusting her dress and trying not to look like she was about to commit a crime.

"Hayley?" Her brother looked at her as if she had grown another head. "What are you doing in my bar?"

"I'm here to have a hamburger. And…a beer."

Ace shook his head. "You don't want beer."

Darn him for being right. She couldn't stand the smell of the stuff, and she'd honestly never even been tempted to taste it.

"No," she agreed. "I want a Coke."

"I will get you a Coke. Are Mom and Dad here?"

She sighed heavily. "No, they're not. I do go places without them. I moved out."

"I know. We talked about it last time Sierra and I went over for dinner."

Hayley's brother had never much cared about his reputation, or about what anyone thought of him. She had been jealous of that for a long time. For years, Ace had been a total hellion and a womanizer, until he'd settled down and married the town rodeo princess, Sierra West. Now the two of them had one child and another on the way, and Ace's position in the community had improved vastly.

"Right. Well, I'm just saying." She traced an imaginary pattern over the bar top with the tip of her finger. "Did I tell you I quit working at the church?"

Ace look surprised by that. "No."

"Well," she said, "I did. I'm working for Jonathan Bear. Helping out with things around the house and in the office."

Ace frowned. "Well, that probably isn't very much fun. He's kind of a grumpy sumbitch."

"I didn't know you knew him all that well."

"He's my future sister-in-law's brother," Ace said, "but no, I don't know him *well*. He's not very sociable. It's not like he comes to the West family gatherings."

"He said he knows you because he buys beer from you."

"That's how everybody knows me," Ace said.

"Except for me."

"You were *trying* to buy beer from me. I'm just not going to sell one to you."

"That's not fair."

"Sure it is," he said, smiling. "Because you don't actually want to buy beer from me. You're just trying to prove a point."

She scowled. She hated that Ace seemed to understand her so well. "Okay, maybe so. I'm kind of proving a point by being here, I guess."

"Well," he said, "it's all right by me."

"Good."

"I kind of wish you would have come on another night, though," he said, "because I have to go. I promised Sierra I would be home early, so I'm about to take off. But I'll tell Jasmine to keep an eye on you."

"I don't need anybody to keep an eye on me."

"Yes," Ace said, laughing, "you do."

Hayley frowned, and plotted how to order a beer when her brother was gone. Ultimately, she decided to stick with Coke, but when the dancing started, she knew that while she might stay away from alcohol, she didn't want to stay seated. She had danced once. And she had liked it.

She was going to do it again.

Jonathan didn't know what in blazes he was doing at Ace's. Sure, he knew what he'd told himself while getting ready, his whole body restless thanks to memories of kissing Hayley.

He had continued to push those thoughts down while pacing around the house, and then, after a while, he'd decided to go out and find someone to hook up with. He didn't do that kind of thing, not anymore. He had a couple of women he called; he didn't go trawling bars. He was too old for that.

But right now, he was too much of a hazard to his innocent assistant, and he needed to take the edge off.

And it occurred to him that if he went to Ace's bar and found somebody, the news might filter back to Hayley.

Even though she might find it upsetting, it would be beneficial in the long run. She didn't want to mess with a man like him, not really. It was only that she was too innocent realize the dangers. But she would, eventually, and she would thank him.

That decision made, he'd hauled his ass down to the bar as quickly as possible.

By the time he walked in, his mood had not improved. He had thought it might. The decision to find a willing woman should have cheered him up. But he felt far from cheered. Maybe because an anonymous body was the last thing he wanted.

He wanted *Hayley*.

Whether he should or not. But he wasn't going to have Hayley. So he would have to get the hell over it.

He moved to the bar and then looked over at the dance floor. His chest tightened up. His body hardened. There was a petite brunette in a formfitting dress dancing with no one in particular. Two men hovered nearby, clearly not minding as she turned to and away from each of them, giving them both just a little bit of attention.

She reminded him of Hayley. Out there on the dance floor acting like nothing close to Hayley.

Then she turned, her dark hair shimmering behind her in a stream, a bright smile on her face, and he could barely process his thoughts. Because it was Hayley. *His* Hayley, out there in the middle of the dance floor, wearing a dress that showed off the figure her clothes had only hinted at before. Sure, in comparison to a lot of women, there was nothing flashy about it, but for Hayley Thompson, it was damned flashy.

And he was… Well, he would be damned if he was going to let those guys put their hands on her.

Yeah, he was bad news. Yeah, he was the kind of guy she should stay well away from. But those guys weren't any better. College douche bags. Probably in their twenties, closer to her age, sure, but not the kind of men who knew how to handle a woman. Especially not one as inexperienced as Hayley.

She would need a man who could guide the experience, show her what she liked. A man who could unlock the mysteries of sex, of her body.

Dickwads that age were better off with an empty dorm room and a half bottle of lotion.

And there was no way in hell they were getting their hands on her.

Without ordering, he moved away from the bar and went out on the dance floor. "You're done here," he said to one of the guys, who looked at him as though Jonathan had just threatened his life. His tone had been soft and even, but it was nice to know the younger man had heard the implied threat loud and clear.

Hayley hadn't noticed his approach, or that the other guy had scurried off to the other end of the dance floor. She was too involved with the guy she was currently dancing with to notice. She was shaking her head, her eyes closed, her body swaying to the music. A completely different kind of dancing than the two of them had done last week.

Then her current dance partner caught Jonathan's eye and paled. He slunk off into the shadows, too.

If Jonathan hadn't already found them wanting when it came to Hayley, he would have now. If they were any kind of men, they would have stood up and declared their interest. They would have proclaimed their desire for her, marked their territory.

He still would have thrown punches, but at least he would've respected them a bit.

Not now.

"Mind if I dance with you?"

Her eyes flew open and she looked around, her

head whipping from side to side, her hair following suit. "Where are…"

"Tweedledee and Tweedledum had somewhere to be."

"Where?"

"Someplace where I wouldn't beat their asses."

"Why are you going to beat their…butts?"

"What are you doing here, Hayley?"

She looked around, a guilty expression on her face. "I was just dancing. I have to say, when I imagined getting in trouble in a bar, I figured it would be my dad dragging me outside, not my boss."

"I haven't dragged you outside. *Yet*." He added that last bit because at this point he wasn't sure how this night was going to end. "What are you doing?"

She lifted a shoulder. "Dancing."

"Getting ready to have your first threesome?"

Her mouth dropped open. "I don't even know how that would work."

He huffed out a laugh. "Look it up. On second thought, don't."

She rolled her eyes like a snotty teenager. "We were just dancing. It wasn't a big deal."

"Little girl, what you don't know about men could fill a library. Men don't *just want to dance*. And men don't *just want to kiss*. You can't play these kinds of games. You don't know the rules. You're going to get yourself into trouble."

"I'm not going to get myself into trouble. Did it

ever occur to you that maybe some men are nicer than you?"

He chuckled, a low, bitter sound. "Oh, I know that most men are a lot nicer than me. Even then, they want in your pants."

"I don't know what your problem is. You don't want me, so what do you care if they do?"

"Hayley, honey, I don't *want* to want you, but that is not the same thing as not wanting you. It is not even close. What I want is something you can't handle."

"I know," she said, looking to the right and then to the left, as though making sure no one was within earshot. Then she took a step toward him. "You said you wanted to…be inside of me."

That simple statement, that repetition of his words, had him hard as an iron bar. "You better back off."

"See, I thought you didn't want me. I thought you were trying to scare me away when you said that. Because why would you want me?"

"I'd list the reasons, but I would shock you."

She tilted her head to the side, her hair falling over her shoulder like a glossy curtain. "Maybe I want to be shocked. Maybe I want something I'm not quite ready for."

"No," he said, his tone emphatic now. "You're on this big kick to have experiences. And there are much nicer men you can have experiences with."

She bared her teeth. "I was trying! You just scared them off."

"You're not having experiences with those clowns. They wouldn't know how to handle a woman if she came with an instruction manual. And let me tell you, women do not come with an instruction manual. You just have to know what to do."

"And you know what to do?"

"Damn straight," he returned.

"So," she said, tilting her chin up, looking stubborn. "Show me."

"Not likely, babe."

He wanted to. He wanted to pick her up, throw her over his shoulder and drag her back to his cave. He wanted to bury himself inside her and screw them both senseless, breathless. He wanted to chase every man in the vicinity away from her. He wanted to make it known, loud and clear that—for a little while at least—she was his.

But it was wrong. On about a thousand levels. And the fact that she didn't seem to know it was just another bit of evidence that he needed to stay away.

"You're playing with fire," he said.

"I know. When you kissed me, that was the closest to being burned I've ever experienced in my life. I want more of that."

"We're not having this conversation in the middle of a bar." He grabbed her arm and hauled her off the dance floor, steering them both to the door.

"Hayley!"

He turned and saw one of the waitresses standing by the bar with her hands on her hips.

"Is everything all right?" she asked.

"Yes," Hayley responded. "Jasmine, it's fine. This is my boss."

Jasmine arched her brow. "Really?"

Hayley nodded. "Really. Just work stuff."

Then she broke free of him and marched out ahead of him. When they were both outside, she rounded on him, her words coming out on a frosty cloud in the night air.

"You're so concerned about my reputation, but then you wander in and make a spectacle."

"You were dancing with two men when I got there," he said. "And what's happening with that dress?"

"Oh please," she said, "I wear this dress to church. It's fine."

"You wear that to *church*?" He supposed, now that he evaluated it with more neutrality, it was pretty tame. The black stretch cotton fell past her knees and had a fairly high neckline. But he could see the curves of her breasts, the subtle slope of her waist to her hips, and her ass looked incredible.

He didn't know if hers was the sort of church that did confession, but he would sure as hell need to confess if he were seated in a row behind her during service.

"Yes," she said. "And it's fine. You're being crazy. Because…because you…*like* me. You *like me* like me."

There she went again, saying things that revealed how innocent she was. Things that made him want her even more, when they should send him running.

"I don't have relationships," he said. He would tell her the truth. He would be honest. It would be the fastest way to chase her off. "And I'm betting a nice girl like you wants a relationship. Wants romance, and flowers, and at least the possibility of commitment. You don't get any of those things with me, Hayley."

She looked up at him, her blue eyes glittering in the security light. He could hear the waves crashing on the shore just beyond the parking lot, feel the salt breeze blowing in off the water, sharp and cold.

"What would I get?" she asked.

"A good, hard fuck. A few orgasms." He knew he'd shocked her, and he was glad. She needed to be shocked. She needed to be scared away.

He couldn't see her face, not clearly, but he could tell she wasn't looking at him when she said, "That's…that's a good thing, right?"

"If you don't know the answer, then the answer is no. Not for you."

The sounds of the surf swelled around them, wind whipping through the pines across the road. She didn't speak for a long time. Didn't move.

"Kiss me again," she said, finally.

The words hit him like a sucker punch. "What? What did I just tell you about men and kissing?"

"It's not for you," she said, "it's for me. Before I give you an answer, you need to kiss me again."

She raised her head, and the light caught her face. She stared at him, all defiance and soft lips, all innocence and intensity, and he didn't have it in him to deny her.

Didn't have it in him to deny himself.

Before he could stop, he wrapped his arm around her waist, crushed her against his chest and brought his lips crashing down on hers.

Seven

She was doing this. She wasn't going to turn back. Not now. And she kept telling herself that as she followed Jonathan's pickup truck down the long, empty highway that took them out of town, toward his house.

His house. Where she was going to spend the night.

Where she was going to lose her virginity.

She swallowed hard, her throat suddenly dry and prickly like a cactus.

This wasn't what she had planned when she'd started on her grand independence journey. Yes, she had wanted a kiss, but she hadn't really thought as far ahead as having a sexual partner. For most of her life she had imagined she would be married first, and then, when she'd started wavering on that decision, she had at least imagined she would be in a serious relationship.

This was… Well, it wasn't marriage. It wasn't the beginning of a relationship, either. Of that, she was certain. Jonathan hadn't been vague. Her cheeks heated at the memory of what he'd said, and she was grateful they were driving in separate cars so she had a moment alone for a private freak-out.

She was so out of her league here.

She could turn around. She could head back to town, back to Main Street, back to her little apartment where she could curl up in bed with the bowl of cereal she'd left dry and discarded on the counter earlier.

And in the morning, she wouldn't be changed. Not for the better, not for the worse.

She seriously considered that, though she kept on driving, her eyes on the road and on Jonathan's taillights.

This decision was a big deal. She wouldn't pretend it wasn't. Wouldn't pretend she didn't put some importance on her first sexual experience, on sex in general. And she wouldn't pretend it probably wasn't a mistake.

It was just that maybe she needed to make the mistake. Maybe she needed to find out for herself if Jonathan was right, if every experience wasn't necessary.

She bit her lip and allowed herself a moment of undiluted honesty. When this was over, there would be fallout. She was certain of it.

But while it was happening, it would feel really, really good.

If the kissing was anything to go by, it would be amazing.

She would feel…wild. And new. And maybe sex with Jonathan would be just the kind of thing she needed. He was hot; touching him burned.

Maybe he could be her own personal trial by fire.

She had always imagined that meant walking through hard times. And maybe, conventionally, it did. But she was walking into the heat willingly, knowing the real pain would come after.

She might be a virgin, but she wasn't an idiot. Jonathan Bear wasn't going to fall in love with her. And anyway, she didn't want him to.

She wanted freedom. She wanted something bigger than Copper Ridge.

That meant love wasn't on her agenda, either.

They pulled up to the house and he got out of his truck, closing the door solidly behind him. And she…froze. Sitting there in the driver's seat, both hands on the steering wheel, the engine still running.

The car door opened and cool air rushed in. She looked up and saw Jonathan's large frame filling the space. "Second thoughts?"

She shook her head. "No," she said, and yet she couldn't make herself move.

"I want you," he said, his voice rough, husky, the words not at all what she had expected. "I would like to tell you that if you are having second thoughts, you should turn the car around and go back home. But I'm not going to tell you that. Because if I do, then I might miss out on my chance. And I want this. Even though I shouldn't."

She tightened her hold on the steering wheel. "Why shouldn't you?" she asked, her throat constricted now.

"Do you want the full list?"

"I've got all night."

"All right. You're a nice girl. You seem to believe the best of people, or at least, you want to, until they absolutely make it so you can't. I'm not a nice man. I don't believe the best of anyone, even when they prove I should. People like me, we tend to drag people like you down to our level. Unfortunately. And that's likely what's going to happen here. I'm going to drag you right down to my level. Because let me tell you, I like dirty. And I'm going to get you filthy. I can promise you that."

"Okay," she said, feeling breathless, not quite certain how to respond. Part of her wanted to fling herself out of the car and into his arms, while another, not insignificant part wanted to throw the car in Reverse and drive away.

"I can only promise you two things. This—you and me—won't last forever. And tonight, I will make you come. If you're okay with those promises, then get out of the car and up to my room. If you're not, it's time for you to go."

For some reason, that softly issued command was what it took to get her moving. She released her hold on the steering wheel and turned sideways in her seat. Then she looked up at him, pushing herself into a standing position. He had one hand on the car door, the other on the side mirror, blocking her in.

Her breasts nearly touched his chest, and she was tempted to lean in and press against him completely.

"Come on then," he said, releasing his hold on the car and turning away.

The movement was abrupt. It made her wonder if he was struggling with indecision, too. Which didn't really make sense, since Jonathan was the most decisive man she had ever met. He seemed certain about everything, all the time, even if he was sure it was a bad decision.

That certainty was what she wanted. Yeah, she was certain this was a bad decision, too, but she was going for it, anyway.

She had walked into this house five days a week for the past couple weeks, yet this time was different. Because this time she wasn't headed to the office. This time she was going to his bedroom. And she wasn't his employee; he wasn't her boss. Not now.

Her stomach tightened, her blood heated at the idea of following orders. His orders. Lord knew she would need instruction. Direction. She had no idea what she was doing; she was just following her gut instinct.

When they reached the long hallway, they stopped at a different door than usual. His bedroom. She had never been inside Jonathan's bedroom. It was strange to be standing there now. So very deliberate.

It might have been easier if they had started kissing here in the house, and let things come to their natural conclusion… On the floor or something. She was reasonably sure people did it on the floor sometimes.

Yeah, that would have been easier. This was so *intentional*.

She was about to say something about the strangeness of it when he reached out, cupped her chin and tilted her face upward. Then he closed the distance between them, claiming her mouth.

She felt his possession, all the way down to her toes.

He didn't wait for her to part her lips this time. Instead, he invaded her, sliding his tongue forcibly against hers, his arms wrapped tight around her like steel bands. There was nothing gentle about this kiss. It was consuming, all-encompassing. And all her thoughts about the situation feeling premeditated dissolved.

This time, she didn't stand there as a passive participant. This time, she wrapped her arms around his neck—pressing her breasts flush against his chest, forking her fingers through his hair—and devoured him right back.

She couldn't believe this was her. Couldn't believe this was her life, that this man wanted her. That he was hard for her. That he thought she might be a mistake, and he was willing to make her, anyway. God knew, she was willing to make him.

Need grew inside her, prowling around like a restless thing. She rocked her hips forward, trying to tame the nameless ache between her thighs. Trying to calm the erratic, reckless feeling rioting through her.

He growled, sliding his hands down her back, over her bottom, down to her thighs. She squeaked as he gripped her tightly, pulling both her feet off the ground and picking her up, pressing that soft, tender place between her legs against his arousal.

"Wrap your legs around me," he said against her mouth, the command harsh, and sexier because of that.

She obeyed him, locking her ankles behind his back. He reversed their positions, pressing her against the wall and deepening his kiss. She gasped as he made even firmer contact with the place that was wet and aching for him.

He ground his hips against her, and her internal

muscles pulsed. An arc of electricity lanced through her. She gripped his shoulders hard, vaguely aware that she might be digging her fingernails into his skin, not really sure that she cared. Maybe it would hurt him, but she wasn't exactly sure if he was hurting her or not. She was suspended between pleasure and pain, feelings so intense she could scarcely breathe.

And through all that, he continued to devour her mouth, the rhythm of his tongue against hers combining with the press of his firm length between her thighs, ensuring that her entire world narrowed down to him. Jonathan Bear was everything right now. He was her breath; he was sensation. He was heaven and he was hell.

She needed it to end. Needed to reach some kind of conclusion, where all this tension could be defused.

And yet she wanted it to go on forever.

Her face was hot, her limbs shaking. A strange, hollow feeling in the pit of her stomach made her want to cry. It was too much. And it was not enough. That sharp, insistent ache between her legs burrowed deeper with each passing second, letting her know this kiss simply wasn't enough at all.

She moved her hands up from his broad shoulders, sliding them as far as she could into his long, dark hair. Her fingers snagged on the band that kept his hair tied back and she internally cursed her clumsiness, hoping he wouldn't notice. She had enthusiasm guiding her through this, but that was about it. Enthusiasm and a healthy dose of adrenaline that bordered on terror. But she didn't want to stop. She couldn't stop.

Those big, rough hands gripped her hips and braced her as he rocked more firmly against her, and suddenly, stars exploded behind her eyes. She gasped, wrenching her lips away from his as something that felt like thunder rolled through her body, muscles she'd never been aware of before pulsing like waves against the shore.

She pressed her forehead against his shoulder, did her best to grit her teeth and keep herself from crying out, but a low, shaky sound escaped when the deepest wave washed over her.

Then it ended, and she felt even more connected to reality, to this moment, than she had a second ago. And she felt…so very aware that she was pressed against the wall and him, that something had just happened, that she hadn't been fully cognizant of her actions. She didn't know what she might have said.

That was when she realized she was digging her nails into his back, and she had probably punctured his skin. She started to move against him, trying to get away, and he gripped her chin again, steadying her. "Hey," he said, "you're not going anywhere."

"I need to… I have to…"

"You don't have to do anything, baby. Nothing at

all. Just relax." She could tell he was placating her. She couldn't bring herself to care particularly, because she needed placating. Her heart was racing, her hands shaking, and that restlessness that had been so all-consuming earlier was growing again. She had thought the earthquake inside her had handled that.

That was when she realized exactly what that earthquake had been.

Her cheeks flamed, horror stealing through her. She'd had… Well, she'd had an orgasm. And he hadn't even touched her. Not with his hands. Not under her clothes.

"I'm sorry," she said, putting her hands up, patting his chest, then curling her hands into fists because she had patted him and that was really stupid. "I'm just sorry."

He frowned. "What are you sorry about?"

"I'm sorry because I—I…I did that. And we didn't…"

He raised one eyebrow. "Are you apologizing for your orgasm?"

She squeezed her eyes tightly shut. "Yes."

"Why?"

She tightened her fists even more, pressing them against her own chest, keeping her eyes closed. "Because we didn't even… You didn't… We're still dressed."

"Honey," he said, taking hold of her fists and

drawing them toward him, pressing them against his chest. "You don't need to apologize to me for coming."

She opened one eye. "I...I don't?"

"No."

"But that..." She looked fully at him, too curious to be embarrassed now. "That ruins it, doesn't it? We didn't..."

"You can have as many orgasms as I can give you. That's the magical thing about women. There's no ceiling on that."

"There isn't?"

"You didn't know?"

"No."

"Hayley," he said, his tone grave, "I need to ask you a question."

Oh great. Now he was actually going to ask if she was a virgin. Granted, she thought he'd probably guessed, but apparently he needed to hear it. "Go ahead," she said, bracing herself for utter humiliation.

"Have you never had an orgasm before?"

"Yes," she said, answering the wrong question before he even got his out. "I mean... No. I mean, just a minute ago. I wasn't even sure what it was right when it was happening."

"That doesn't... Not even with yourself?"

Her face felt so hot she thought it might be on fire. She was pretty sure her heart was beating in her forehead. "No." She shook her head. "I can't talk to you about things like that."

"I just gave you your first orgasm, so you better be able to talk to me about things like that. Plus I'm aiming to give you another one before too long here."

"I bet you can't."

He chuckled, and then he bent down, sweeping her up into his arms. She squeaked, curling her fingers around his shirt. "You should know better than to issue challenges like that." He turned toward the bedroom door, kicking it open with his boot before walking inside and kicking it closed again. Then he carried her to the bed and threw her down in the center.

"Wait," she said, starting to feel panicky, her heart fluttering in her chest like a swarm of butterflies. "Just wait a second."

"I'm not going to fall on you like a ravenous beast," he said, his hands going to the top button of his shirt. "Yet." He started to undo the button slowly, revealing his tan, muscular chest.

She almost told him to stop, except he stripped the shirt off, and she got completely distracted by the play of all those muscles. The sharp hitch of his abs as he cast the flannel onto the floor, the shift and bunch of his pectoral muscles as he pushed his hand over his hair.

She had never seen a shirtless man that looked

like him. Not in person, anyway. And most definitely not this close, looking at her like he had plans. Very, very dirty plans.

"I'm a virgin," she blurted out. "Just so you know."

His eyes glowed with black fire. For one heart-stopping moment she was afraid he might pick up his shirt and walk out of the room. His eyes looked pure black; his mouth pressed into a firm line. He stood frozen, hands on his belt buckle, every line in his cut torso still.

Then something in his expression shifted. Nearly imperceptible, and mostly unreadable, but she had seen it. Then his deft fingers went to work, moving his belt through the buckle. "I know," he said.

"Oh." She felt a little crestfallen. Like she must have made some novice mistake and given herself away.

"You're a church secretary who confessed to having never had an orgasm. I assumed." He lowered his voice. "If you hadn't told me outright, I could have had plausible deniability. Which I was sort of counting on."

She blinked. "Did you…need it?"

"My conscience is screwed, anyway. So not really."

She didn't know quite what to say, so she didn't say anything.

"Have you ever seen a naked man before?"

She shook her head. "No."

"Pictures?"

"Does medieval art count?"

"No, it does not."

"Then no," she said, shaking her head even more vigorously.

He rubbed his hand over his forehead, and she was sure she heard him swear beneath his breath. "Okay," he said, leaving his belt hanging open, but not going any further. He pressed his knee down on the mattress, kneeling beside her. Then he took her hand and placed it against his chest. "How's that?"

She drew shaking fingers across his chest slowly, relishing his heat, the satiny feel of his skin. "Good," she said. "You're very…hot. I mean, temperature-wise. Kind of smooth."

"You don't have to narrate," he said.

"Sorry," she said, drawing her hand back sharply.

"No," he said, pressing her palm back against his skin. "Don't apologize. Don't apologize for anything that happens between us tonight, got that?"

"Okay," she said, more than happy to agree, but not entirely sure if she could keep to the agreement. Because every time she moved her hand and his breath hissed through his teeth, she wanted to say she was sorry. Every time she took her exploration further, she wanted to apologize for the impulse to do it.

She bit her lip, letting her hands glide lower, over his stomach, which was as hard and rippled as corrugated steel. Then she found her hands at the waistband of his jeans, and she pulled back.

"Do you want me to take these off?" he asked.

"In a minute," she said, losing her nerve slightly. "Just a minute." She rose up on her knees, pressed her mouth to his and lost herself in kissing him. She really liked kissing. Loved the sounds he made, loved being enveloped in his arms, and she really loved it when he laid them both down, pressing her deep into the mattress and settling between her thighs.

Her dress rode up high, and she didn't care. She felt rough denim scraping her bare skin, felt the hard press of his zipper, and his arousal behind it through the thin fabric of her panties.

She lost herself in those sensations. In the easy, sensual contact that pushed her back to the brink again. She could see already that Jonathan was going to win the orgasm challenge. And she was okay with that.

Very, very okay with that.

Then he took her hem and pulled the cotton dress over her head, casting it onto the floor. Her skin heated all over, and she was sure she was pink from head to toe.

"Don't be embarrassed," he said, touching her collarbone, featherlight, then tracing a trail down to the curve of her breast, to the edge of her bra. "You're beautiful."

She didn't know quite how to feel about that. Didn't know what to do with that husky, earnest compliment. She wasn't embarrassed because she lacked beauty, but because she had always been taught to treasure modesty. To respect her body, to save it.

He *was* respecting it, though. And right now, she felt like she had been saving it for him.

He reached behind her, undoing her bra with one hand and flicking the fabric to the side.

"You're better at that than I am," she said, laughing nervously as he bared her breasts, her nipples tightening as the cold air hit her skin.

He smiled. "You'll appreciate that in a few minutes."

"What will I appreciate?" she asked, shivering. She crossed her arms over her chest.

"My skill level." Instead of moving her hands, he bent his head and nuzzled the tender spot right next to her hand, the full part of her breast that was still exposed. She gasped, tightening her hold on herself.

He was not deterred.

He nosed her gently and shifted her hand to the side, pressing a kiss to her skin, sending electric sensations firing through her. "Don't be shy," he said, "not with me."

She waited for a reason why. He didn't give one, but she found that the more persistent he was—the more hot, open-mouthed kisses he pressed to her skin—the less able she was to deny him anything. Anything at all. She found herself shifting her hands and then letting them fall away.

As soon as she did, he closed his lips over her nipple, sucking deep. She gasped, her hips rocking up off the bed. He wrapped his arm around her, holding her against his hardness as he teased her with his lips and tongue.

Every time she wiggled, either closer to him, or in a moment of self-consciousness, away, it only brought him more in contact with that aching place between her thighs, and then she would forget why she was moving at all. Why she wasn't just letting him take the lead.

So she relaxed into him, and let herself get lost. She was in a daze when he took her hand and pushed it down his stomach, to the front of his jeans. She gasped when his hard, denim-covered length filled her palm.

"Feel that? That's how much I want you. That's what you do to me."

A strange surge of power rocketed through her. That she could cause such a raw, sexual response... Well, it was intoxicating in a way she hadn't appreciated it could be.

Especially because he was such a man. A hot man. A sexy man, and she had never thought of anyone that way in her life. But he was. He most definitely was.

"Are you ready?" he asked.

She nodded, sliding her hand experimentally over him. He moved, undoing his pants and shoving them quickly down, hardly giving her a chance to prepare. Her mouth dried when she saw him, all of him. She hadn't really... Well, she had been content to allow her fantasies to be somewhat hazy. Though reading that romance novel had made those fantasies a little sharper.

Still, she hadn't really imagined specifically how large a man might be. But suffice it to say, he was a bit larger than she had allowed for.

Her breath left her lungs in a rush. But along with the wave of nerves that washed over her came a sense of relief. "You are... I like the way you look," she said finally.

A crooked smile tipped his mouth upward. "Thank you."

"I told you, I've never seen a naked man before. I was a little afraid I wouldn't like it."

"Well, I'm glad you do. Because let me tell you, that's a lot of pressure. Being the first naked man you've ever seen." His eyes darkened and his voice got lower, huskier. "Being the first naked man you've ever touched." He took her hand again and placed it around his bare shaft, the skin there hotter and much softer than she had imagined. She slid her thumb up and down, marveling at the feel of him.

"You're the first man I've ever kissed," she said, the words slurred, because she had lost the full connection between her brain and her mouth. All her blood had flowed to her extremities.

He swore, and then crushed her to him, kissing her deeply and driving her back down to the mattress. His erection pressed into her stomach, his tongue slick against hers, his lips insistent. She barely noticed when he divested her of her underwear, until he placed his hand between her legs. The rough pads of his fingers sliding through her slick flesh, the white-hot pleasure his touch left behind, made her gasp.

"I'm going to make sure you're ready," he said.

She had no idea what that meant. But he started doing wicked, magical things with his fingers, so she didn't much care. Then he slid one finger deep inside her and she arched away, not sure whether she wanted more of that completely unfamiliar sensation, or if she needed to escape it.

"It's okay," he said, moving his thumb in a circle over a sensitive bundle of nerves as he continued to slide his finger in and out of her body.

After a few passes of his thumb, she agreed.

He shifted his position, adding a second finger, making her gasp. It burned slightly, made her feel like she was being stretched, but after a moment, she adjusted to that, too.

That lovely, spiraling tension built inside her again, and she knew she was close to the edge. But every time he took her to the brink, he would drop back again.

"Please," she whispered.

"Please what?" he asked, being dastardly, asking her to clarify, when he knew saying the words would embarrass her.

"You know," she said, placing her hand over his, like she might take control, increase the pressure, increase the pace, since he refused.

But, of course, he was too strong for her to guide him at all. "I need to hear it."

"I need… I need to have an orgasm," she said quickly.

For a moment, he stopped. He looked at her like she mystified him. Like he had never seen anything like her before. Then he withdrew his hand and slid down her body, gripping her hips roughly before drawing her quickly against his mouth.

She squeaked when his lips and tongue touched her right in her most intimate place. She reached down, grabbing hold of his hair, because she was going to pull him away, but then his tongue touched her in the most amazing spot and she found herself lacing her fingers through his hair instead.

She found herself holding him against her instead of pushing him away.

She moved her hips in time with him, gasping for air as pleasure, arousal, built to impossible heights. She had been on the edge for so long now it felt like she was poised on the brink of something else entirely. But right when she was about to break, he moved away from her, drawing himself up her body.

He grabbed a small, round packet from the bed-spread that she hadn't noticed until now, and tore it open, quickly sheathing himself before moving to position the blunt head of his arousal at her entrance.

He flexed his hips, thrusting deep inside her, and her arousal broke like a mirror hit with a hammer. She gritted her teeth as pain—sharp and jagged—cut through all the hidden places within her. But along with the pain came the intense sensation of being full. Of being connected to another person like she never had been before.

She reached up, taking his heavily muscled arms and holding him, just holding him, as he moved slowly inside her.

He was *inside* her.

She marveled at that truth even as the pain eased, even as pleasure began to push its way into the fore-ground again.

"Move with me," he said, nuzzling her neck, kiss-ing the tender skin there.

So she did, meeting his every thrust, clinging to him. She could see the effort it took for him to maintain control, and she could see when his con-trol began to fray. When his thrusts became erratic, his golden skin slick with sweat, his breathing rough and ragged, matching her own.

When he thrust deep, she arched her hips, an electric shower of sparks shimmering through her each time.

His hands were braced on either side of her shoulders, his strong fingers gripping the sheets. His movements became hard, rough, but none of the earlier pain remained, and she welcomed him. Opened her thighs wider and then wrapped her legs around his lean hips so she could take him even deeper.

There was no pain. There was no shame. There was no doubt at all.

As far as she was concerned, there was only the two of them.

He leaned down, pressing his forehead against hers, his dark gaze intense as his rhythm increased. He went shallow, then deep, the change pushing her even closer to the edge.

Then he pulled out almost completely, his hips pulsing slightly. The denial of that deep, intimate contact made her feel frantic. Made her feel needy. Made her feel desperate.

"Jonathan," she said. "Jonathan, please."

"Tell me you want to come," he told her, the words a growl.

"I want to come," she said, not wasting a moment on self-consciousness.

He slammed back home, and she saw stars. This orgasm grabbed her deep, reached places she hadn't known were there. The pleasure seemed to go on and on, and when it was done, she felt like she was floating on a sea, gazing up at a sky full of infinite stars.

She felt adrift, but only for a moment. Because

when she came back to herself, she was still clutching his strong arms, Jonathan Bear rooting her to the earth.

And then she waited.

Waited for regret. Waited for guilt.

But she didn't feel any of it. Right now, she just felt a bone-deep satisfaction she hoped never went away.

"I…" He started to say something, moving away from her. Then he frowned. "You don't have a toothbrush or anything, do you?"

It was such a strange question that it threw her for a loop. "What?"

"It doesn't matter," he said. He bent down, pressing a kiss to her forehead. "We'll work something out in the morning."

She was glad he'd said there was nothing to worry about, because her head was starting to get fuzzy and her eyelids were heavy. Which sucked, because she didn't want to sleep. She wanted to bask in her newfound warm and fuzzy feelings.

But she was far too sleepy, far too sated to do anything but allow herself to be enveloped by that warmth. By him.

He drew her into his arms, and she snuggled into his chest, pressing her palm against him. She could feel his heartbeat, hard and steady, beneath her hand.

And then, for the first time in her life, Hayley Thompson fell asleep in a man's arms.

Eight

Jonathan didn't sleep. As soon as Hayley drifted off, he went into his office, busying himself with work that didn't need to be done.

Women didn't spend the night at his house. He had never even brought a woman back to this house. But when Hayley had looked up at him like that… He hadn't been able to tell her to leave. He realized that she expected to stay. Because as far as she was concerned, sex included sleeping with somebody.

He had no idea where she had formed her ideas about relationships, but they were innocent. And he was a bastard. He had already known that, but to-night just confirmed it.

Except he had let her stay.

He couldn't decide if that was a good thing or not. Couldn't decide if letting her stay had been a kindness or a cruelty. Because the one thing it hadn't been was the reality of the situation.

The reality was this wasn't a relationship. The reality was, it had been... Well, a very bad idea.

He stood up from his desk, rubbing the back of his neck. It was getting light outside, pale edges beginning to bleed from the mountaintops, encroaching on the velvet middle of the sky.

He might as well go outside and get busy on morning chores. And if some of those chores were in the name of avoiding Hayley, then so be it.

He made his way downstairs, shoved his feet into his boots and grabbed his hat, walking outside with heavy footsteps.

He paused, inhaling deeply, taking a moment to let the scent of the pines wash through him. This was his. All of it was his. He didn't think that revelation would ever get old.

He remembered well the way it had smelled on his front porch in the trailer park. Cigarette smoke and exhaust from cars as people got ready to leave for work. The noise of talking, families shouting at each other. It didn't matter if you were inside the house or outside. You lived way too close to your neighbors to avoid them.

He had fantasized about a place like this back then. Isolated. His. Where he wouldn't have to see another person unless he went out of his way to do so. He shook his head. And he had gone and invited Hayley to stay the night. He was a dumb ass.

He needed a ride to clear his head. The fact that he got to take weekends off now was one of his favorite things about his new position in life. He was a workaholic, and he had never minded that. But ranching was the kind of work he really enjoyed, and that was what he preferred to do with his free time.

He saddled his horse and mounted up, urging the bay gelding toward the biggest pasture. They started out at a slow walk, then Jonathan increased the pace until he and his horse were flying over the grass, patches of flowers blurring on either side of them, blending with the rich green.

It didn't matter what mess he had left behind at the house. Didn't matter what mistakes he had made last night. It never did, not when he was on a horse. Not when he was in his sanctuary. The house… Well, he would be lying if he said that big custom house hadn't been a goal for him. Of course it had been. It was evidence that he had made it.

But this… The trees, the mountains, the wind in his face, being able to ride his horse until his lungs burned, and not reach the end of his property… That was the real achievement. It belonged to him and no one else. In this place he didn't have to answer to anyone.

Out here it didn't matter if he was bad. You

couldn't let the sky down. You couldn't disappoint the mountains.

He leaned forward to go uphill, tightening his hold on the reins as the animal changed its gait. He pulled back, easing to a stop. He looked down the mountain, at the valley of trees spread out before him, an evergreen patchwork stitched together by rock and river. And beyond that, the ocean, brighter blue than usual on this exceptionally clear morning, the waves capped with a rosy pink handed down from the still-rising sun.

Hayley would love this.

That thought brought him up short, because he wasn't exactly sure why he thought she would. Or why he cared. Why he suddenly wanted to show her. He had never shown this view to anybody. Not even to his sister, Rebecca.

He had wanted to keep it for himself, because growing up, he'd had very little that belonged to him and him alone. In fact, up here, gazing at everything that belonged to him now, he couldn't think of a single damn thing that had truly belonged to him when he'd been younger.

It had all been for a landlord, for his sister, for the future.

This was what he had worked for his entire life.

He didn't need to show it to some woman he'd slept with last night.

He shook his head, turning the horse around and

trotting down the hill, moving to a gallop back down to the barn.

When he exited the gate that would take him out of the pasture and back to the paddock, Jonathan saw Hayley standing in the path. Wearing last night's dress, her hair disheveled, she was holding two mugs of coffee.

He was tempted to imagine he had conjured her up just by thinking of her up on the ridge. But if it were a fantasy, she would have been wearing nothing, rather than being back in that black cotton contraption.

She was here, and it disturbed him just how happy that made him.

"I thought I might find you out here," she said. "And I figured you would probably want your coffee."

He dismounted, taking the reins and walking the horse toward Hayley. "It's your day off. You don't have to make me coffee."

Her cheeks turned pink, and he marveled at the blush. And on the heels of that marveling came the sharp bite of guilt. She was a woman who blushed routinely. And he had... Well, he had started down the path of corrupting her last night.

He had taken her virginity. Before her he'd never slept with a virgin in his damn life. In high school, that hadn't been so much out of a sense of honor as it had been out of a desire not to face down an angry dad with a shotgun. Better to associate with girls who had reputations worse than his own.

All that restraint had culminated in him screwing the pastor's daughter.

At least when people came with torches and pitchforks, he would have a decent-sized fortress to hole up in.

"I just thought maybe it would be nice," she said finally, taking a step toward him and extending the coffee mug in his direction.

"It is," he said, taking the cup, knowing he didn't sound quite as grateful as he might have. "Sorry," he conceded, sipping the strong brew, which was exactly the way he liked it. "I'm not used to people being nice. I'm never quite sure what to make of it when you are."

"Just take it at face value," she said, lifting her shoulder.

"Yeah, I don't do that."

"Why not?" she asked.

"I have to take care of the horse," he said. "If you want story time, you're going to have to follow me."

He thought his gruff demeanor might scare her off, but instead, she followed him along the fence line. He tethered his horse and set his mug on the fence post, then grabbed the pick and started on the gelding's hooves.

Hayley stepped up carefully on the bottom rung of the fence, settling herself on the top rung, clutching her mug and looking at him with an intensity he could feel even with his focus on the task at hand.

"I'm ready," she said.

He looked up at her, perched there like an inquisitive owl, her lips at the edge of her cup, her blue eyes round. She was…a study in contradictions. Innocent as hell. Soft in some ways, but determined in others.

It was her innocence that allowed her to be so open—that was his conclusion. The fact that she'd never really been hurt before made it easy for her to come at people from the front.

"It's not a happy story," he warned.

It wasn't a secret one, either. Pretty much everybody knew his tragic backstory. He didn't go around talking about it, but there was no reason not to give her what she was asking for.

Except for the fact that he never talked to the women he hooked up with. There was just no point to it.

But then, the women he usually hooked up with never stumbled out of his house early in the morning with cups of coffee. So he supposed it was an unusual situation all around.

"I'm a big girl," she said, her tone comically serious. It was followed by a small slurp as she took another sip of coffee. The sound should not have been cute, but it was.

"Right." He looked up at her, started to speak and then stopped.

Would hearing about his past, about his childhood, change something in her? Just by talking to her he might ruin some of her optimism.

It was too late for worrying about that, he supposed. Since sleeping with her when she'd never even kissed anyone before had undoubtedly changed her.

There had been a lot of points in his life when he had not been his own favorite person. The feeling was intense right now. He was a damned bastard.

"I'm waiting," she said, kicking her foot slightly to signify her impatience.

"My father left when I was five," he said.

"Oh," she said, blinking, clearly shocked. "I'm sorry."

"It was the best thing that had happened to me in all five years of my life, Hayley. The very best thing. He was a violent bastard. He hit my mother. He hit me. The day he left… I was a kid, but I knew even then that life was going to be better. I was right. When I was seven, my mom had another kid. And she was the best thing. So cute. Tiny and loud as hell, but my mother wasn't all that interested in me, and my new sister was. Plus she gave me, I don't know…a feeling of importance. I had someone to look after, and that mattered. Made me feel like maybe I mattered."

"Rebecca," Hayley said.

"Yeah," he replied. "Then, when Rebecca was a teenager, she was badly injured in a car accident.

Needed a lot of surgeries, skin grafts. All of it was paid for by the family responsible for the accident, in exchange for keeping everything quiet. Of course, it's kind of an open secret now that Gage West was the one who caused the accident."

Hayley blinked. "Gage. Isn't she… Aren't they… Engaged?"

Familiar irritation surged through him. "For now. We'll see how long that lasts. I don't have a very high opinion of that family."

"Well, you know my brother is married into that family."

He shrugged. "All right, maybe I'll rephrase that. I don't have anything against Colton, or Sierra, or Maddy. But I don't trust Gage or his father one bit. I certainly don't trust him with my sister, any more now than I did then. But if things fall apart, if he ends up breaking off the engagement, or leaves her ten years into the marriage… I'll have a place for her. I've always got a place for her."

Hayley frowned. "That's a very cynical take. If Rebecca can love the man who caused her accident, there must be something pretty exceptional about him."

"More likely, my sister doesn't really know what love looks like," he said, his voice hard, the words giving voice to the thing he feared most. "I have to backtrack a little. A few months after the accident, my mom took the cash payout Nathan West gave her and took off. Left me with Rebecca. Left Rebecca without a mother, when she needed her mother the most. My mom just couldn't handle it. So I had to. And I was a piss-poor replacement for parents. An older brother with a crappy construction job and not a lot of patience." He shook his head. "Every damn person in my life who was supposed to be there for me bailed. Everyone who was supposed to be there for Rebecca."

"And now you're mad at her, too. For not doing what you thought she should."

Guilt stabbed him right in the chest. Yeah, he was angry at his sister. And he felt like he had no damn right to be angry. Shouldn't she be allowed to be happy? Hadn't that been the entire point of taking care of her for all those years? So she could get out from under the cloud of their family?

So she'd done it. In a huge, spectacular way. She'd ended up with the man she'd been bitter about for years. She had let go of the past. She had embraced it, and in a pretty damned literal way.

But Jonathan couldn't. He didn't trust in sudden changes of heart or professions of love. He didn't trust much of anything.

"I'll be mad if she gets hurt," he said finally. "But that's my default. I assume it's going to end badly because I've only ever seen these things end badly. I worked my ass off to keep the two of us off the streets. To make sure we had a roof over our heads, as much food in our stomachs as I could manage. I protected her." He shook his head. "And there's no protecting somebody if you aren't always looking out for what might go wrong. For what might hurt them."

"I guess I can't blame you for not trusting the good in people. You haven't seen it very many times."

He snorted. "Understatement of the century." He straightened, undoing the girth and taking the saddle off the bay in a fluid movement, then draping it over the fence. "But my cynicism has served me just fine. Look at where I am now. I started out in a single-wide trailer, and I spent years working just to keep that much. I didn't advance to this place by letting down my guard, by stopping for even one minute." He shook his head again. "I probably owe my father a thank-you note. My mother, too, come to that. They taught me that I couldn't trust anyone but myself. And so far that lesson's served me pretty well."

Hayley was looking at him like she was sad for him, and he wanted to tell her to stop it. Contempt, disgust and distrust were what he was used to getting from people. And he had come to revel in that reaction, to draw strength from it.

Pity had been in short supply. And if it was ever tossed in his general direction, it was mostly directed at Rebecca. He wasn't comfortable receiving it himself.

"Don't look at me like I'm a sad puppy," he said.

"I'm not," she returned.

He untied the horse and began to walk back into the barn. "You are. I didn't ask for your pity." He unhooked the lead rope and urged the gelding into his stall. "Don't go feeling things for me, Hayley. I don't deserve it. In fact, what you should have done this morning was walked out and slapped me in the face, not given me a cup of coffee."

"Why?"

"Because I took advantage of you last night. And you should be upset about that."

She frowned. "I should be?" She blinked. "I'm not. I thought about it. And I'm not."

"I don't know what you're imagining this is. I don't know what you think might happen next..."

She jumped down from the fence and set her coffee cup on the ground. Then she took one quick step forward. She hooked an arm around his neck and pushed herself onto her tiptoes, pressing her lips to his.

He was too stunned to react. But only for a moment. He wrapped an arm around her waist, pressing his forefinger beneath her chin and urging the kiss deeper.

She didn't have a lot of skill. That had been apparent the first and second times they'd kissed. And when they had come together last night. But he didn't need skill, he just needed her.

Even though it was wrong, he consumed her, sated his hunger on her mouth.

She whimpered, a sweet little sound that only fueled the driving hunger roaring in his gut. He grabbed her hair, tilting her head back farther, abandoning her mouth to scrape his teeth over her chin and down her neck, where he kissed her again, deep and hard.

He couldn't remember ever feeling like this before. Couldn't remember ever wanting a woman so much it was beyond the need for air. Sure, he liked sex. He was a man, after all. But the need had never been this specific. Had never been for one woman in particular.

But what he was feeling wasn't about sex, or about lust or desire. It was about her. About Hayley. The sweet little sounds she made when he kissed the tender skin on her neck, when he licked his way back up to her lips. The way she trembled with her need for him. The way she had felt last night, soft and slick and made only for him.

This was beyond anything he had ever experienced before. And he was a man who had experienced a hell of a lot.

That's what it was, he thought dimly as he scraped his teeth along her lower lip. And that said awful things about him, but then so did a lot of choices in his life.

He had conducted business with hard, ruthless precision, and he had kept his personal life free of any kind of connection beyond Rebecca—who he was loyal to above anyone else.

So maybe that was the problem. Now that he'd arrived at this place in life, he was collecting those things he had always denied himself. The comfortable home, the expansive mountains and a sweet woman.

Maybe this was some kind of latent urge. He had the homestead, now he wanted to put a woman in it.

He shook off that thought and all the rest. He didn't want to think right now. He just wanted to feel. Wanted to embrace the heat firing through his veins, the need stoking the flame low in his gut, which burned even more with each pass of her tongue against his.

She pulled away from him, breathing hard, her pupils dilated, her lips swollen and rounded into a perfect O. "That," she said, breathlessly, "was what I was thinking might happen next. And that we might… Take me back to bed, please."

"I can't think of a single reason to refuse," he said—a lie, as a litany of reasons cycled through his mind.

But he wasn't going to listen to them. He was going to take her, for as long as she was on offer. And when it ended, he could only hope he hadn't damaged her too much. Could only hope he hadn't broken her beyond repair.

Because there were a couple things he knew for sure. It would end; everything always did. And he would be the one who destroyed it.

He just hoped he didn't destroy her, too.

Nine

It was late in the afternoon when Hayley and Jonathan finally got back out of bed. Hayley felt… Well, she didn't know quite what she felt. Good. Satisfied. Jonathan was… Well, if she'd ever had insecurities about whether or not she might be desirable to a man, he had done away with those completely. He had also taught her things about herself—about pleasure, about her own body—that she'd never in her wildest dreams conceived of.

She didn't know what would happen next, though. She had fallen asleep after their last time together, and when she'd awoken he was gone again. This morning, she had looked for him. She wasn't sure if she should do that twice.

Still, before she could even allow herself to ponder making the decision, she got out of bed, grabbed his T-shirt from the floor and pulled it over her head. Then she padded down the hallway, hoping he didn't have any surprise visitors. That would be a nightmare. Getting caught wearing only a T-shirt in her boss's hallway. There would be a lot of questions about what they had just spent the last few hours doing, that was for sure.

She wondered if Jonathan might be outside again, but she decided to check his office first. And was rewarded when she saw him sitting at the computer, his head lowered over the keyboard, some of his dark hair falling over his face after coming loose from the braid he normally kept it in.

Her heart clenched painfully, and it disturbed her that her heart was the first part of her body to tighten. The rest of her followed shortly thereafter, but she really wished her reaction was more about her body than her feelings. She couldn't afford to have feelings for him. She wasn't staying in Copper Ridge. And even if she were, he wouldn't want her long-term, anyway.

She took a deep breath, trying to dispel the strange, constricted feeling that had overtaken her lungs. "I thought I might find you here," she said.

He looked up, his expression betraying absolutely no surprise. He sneaked up on her all the time, but of course, as always, Jonathan was unflappable. "I just had a few schematics to check over." He pushed the chair away from the desk and stood, reaching over his head to stretch.

She was held captive by the sight of him. Even fully dressed, he was a beautiful thing.

His shoulders and chest were broad and muscular, his waist trim. His face like sculpted rock, or hardened bronze, uncompromising. But she knew the secret way to make those lips soften. Only for her.

No, not only for you. He does this all the time. They are just softening for you right now.

It was good for her to remember that.

"I'm finished now," he said, treating her to a smile that made her feel like melting ice cream on a hot day.

"Good," she said, not quite sure why she said it, because it wasn't like they had made plans. She wondered when he would ask her to leave. Or maybe he wanted her to leave, but didn't want to tell her. "It's late," she said. "I could go."

"Do you need to go?"

"No," she said, a little too quickly.

"Then don't."

Relief washed over her, and she did her best not to show him just how pleased she was by that statement. "Okay," she said, "then I won't go."

"I was thinking. About your list."

She blinked. "My list?"

"Yeah, your list. You had dancing on there. Pretty

sure you had a kiss. And whether or not it was on the list…you did lose your virginity. Since I helped you with those items, I figured I might help you with some of the others."

A deep sense of pleasure and something that felt a lot like delight washed through her. "Really?"

"Yes," he said, "really. I figure we started all of this, so we might as well keep going."

"I don't have an official list."

"Well, that's ridiculous. If you're going to do this thing, you have to do it right." He grabbed a sheet of paper out of the printer and settled back down in the office chair. "Let's make a list."

He picked up a pen and started writing.

"What are you doing? I didn't tell you what I wanted yet."

"I'm writing down what we already did so you have the satisfaction of checking those off."

Her stomach turned over. "Don't write down all of it."

"Oh," he said, "I am. All of it. In detail."

"No!" She crossed the space between them and stood behind him, wrapping her arms around his broad shoulders as if she might restrain him. He kept on writing. She peered around his head, then slapped the pen out of his hand when she saw him writing a very dirty word. "Stop it. If anybody finds that list I could be…incriminated."

He laughed and swiveled the chair to the side.

He wrapped his arm around her waist and pulled her onto his lap. "Oh no. We would hate for you to be incriminated. But on the other hand, the world would know you spent the afternoon with a very firm grip on my—"

"No!"

He looked at her and defiantly put a checkmark by what he had just written. She huffed, but settled into his hold. She liked this too much. Him smiling, him holding her when they had clothes on as if he just wanted to hold her.

It was nice to have him want her in bed. Very nice. But this was something else, and it was nice, too.

"Okay, so we have dancing, kissing, sex, and all of the many achievements beneath the sex," he said, ignoring her small noises of protest. "So what else?"

"I want to go to a place where I need a passport," she said.

"We could drive to Canada."

She laughed. "I was thinking more like Europe. But… Could we really drive to Canada?"

"Well," he said, "maybe not today, since I have to be back here by Monday."

"That's fine. I was thinking more Paris than Vancouver."

"Hey, they speak French in Canada."

"Just write it down," she said, poking his shoulder.

"Fine. What next?"

"I feel like I should try alcohol," she said slowly. "Just so I know."

"Fair enough." He wrote *get hammered*.

"That is not what I said."

"Sorry. I got so excited about the idea of getting you drunk. Lowering your inhibitions."

She rolled her eyes. "I'm already more un-inhibited with you than I've ever been with anyone else." It was true, she realized, as soon as she said it. She was more herself with Jonathan than she had ever been with anyone, including her family, who had known her for her entire life.

Maybe it was the fact that, in a town full of people who were familiar with her, at least by reputation, he was someone she hadn't known at all until a couple weeks ago.

Maybe it was the fact that he had no expectations of her beyond what they'd shared. Whatever the case, around him she felt none of the pressure that she felt around other people in the community.

No need to censor herself, or hide; no need to be respectable or serene when she felt like being disreputable and wild.

"I want to kiss in the rain," she said.

"Given weather patterns," he said slowly, "we should be able to accomplish that, too."

She was ridiculously pleased he wanted to be a part of that, pleased that he hadn't said anything about her finding a guy to kiss in the rain in Paris.

She shouldn't be happy he was assuming he would
be the person to help her fulfill these things. She
should be annoyed. She should feel like he was
inserting himself into her independence, but she
didn't. Mostly because he made her independence
seem…well, like *more*.

"You're very useful, aren't you?"

He looked at her, putting his hand on her cheek,
his dark gaze serious as it met hers. "I'm glad I can
be useful to you."

She felt him getting hard beneath her backside,
and that pleased her, too. "Parts of you are very useful," she said, reaching behind her and slowly stroking his length.

The light in his eyes changed, turning much more
intense. "Hayley Thompson," he said, "I would say
that's shocking behavior."

"I would say you're responsible, Jonathan Bear."

He shook his head. "No, princess, you're responsible for this. For all of this. This is you. It's what you
want, right? The things on your list that you don't
even want to write down. It's part of you. You don't
get to blame it all on me."

She felt strangely empowered by his words. By
the idea that this was her, and not just him leading
her somewhere.

"That's very… Well, that's very… I like it." She
furthered her exploration of him, increasing the
pressure of her touch. "At least, I like it with you."

"I'm not complaining."

"That's good," she said softly, continuing to stroke him through the fabric of his pants.

She looked down, watched herself touching him. It was…well, now that she had started, she didn't want to stop.

"I would be careful if I were you," he said, his tone laced with warning, "because you're about to start something, and it's very likely you need to take a break from all that."

"Do I? Why would I need a break?"

"Because you're going to get sore," he said, maddeningly pragmatic.

And, just as maddeningly, it made her blush to hear him say it. "I don't really mind," she said finally.

"You don't?" His tone was calm, but heat flared in the depths of his dark eyes.

"No," she replied, still trailing her fingertips over his hardening body. "I like feeling the difference. In me. I like being so…aware of everything we've done." For her, that was a pretty brazen proclamation, though she had a feeling it paled in comparison to the kinds of things other women had said to him in the past.

But she wasn't one of those other women. And right now he was responding to her, so she wasn't going to waste a single thought on anyone who had come before her. She held his interest now. That was enough.

"There's something else on my list," she said, fighting to keep her voice steady, fighting against the nerves firing through her.

"Is that so?"

She sucked in a sharp breath. "Yes. I want to… That is… What you did for me… A couple of times now… I want to… I want to…" She gave up trying to get the words out. She wasn't sure she had the right words for what she wanted to do, anyway, and she didn't want to humiliate herself by saying something wrong.

So, with unsteady hands, she undid the closure on his jeans and lowered the zipper. She looked up at him. If she expected to get any guidance, she was out of luck. He just stared at her, his dark eyes unfathomable, his jaw tight, a muscle in his cheek ticking.

She shifted on his lap, sliding gracefully to the floor in front of the chair. Then she went to her knees and turned to face him, flicking her hair out of her face.

He still said nothing, watching her closely, unnervingly so. But she wasn't going to turn back now. She lifted the waistband of his underwear, pulling it out in order to clear his impressive erection, then she pulled the fabric partway down his hips, as far as she could go with him sitting.

He was beautiful.

That feeling of intimidation she'd felt the first time she'd seen him had faded completely. Now she knew what he could do, and she appreciated it greatly. He had shown her so many things; he'd made her pleasure the number one priority. And she wanted to give to him in return.

Well, she also knew this would be for her, too.

She slid her hands up his thighs, then curled her fingers around his hardened length, squeezing him firmly. She was learning that he wasn't breakable there. That he liked a little bit of pressure.

"Hayley," he said, his voice rough, "I don't think you know what you're doing."

"No," she said, "I probably don't. But I know what I want. And it's been so much fun having what I want." She rose up slightly, then leaned in, pressing her lips to the head of his shaft. He jerked beneath her touch, and she took that as approval.

A couple hours ago she would have been afraid that she'd hurt him. But male pleasure, she was discovering, sometimes looked a little like pain. Heck, female pleasure was a little like pain. Sex was somewhere between. The aching need to have it all and the intense rush of satisfaction that followed.

She shivered just thinking about it.

And then she flicked her tongue out, slowly testing this new territory. She hummed, a low sound in the back of her throat, as she explored the taste of him, the texture. Jonathan Bear was her favorite indulgence, she was coming to realize. There was nothing about him she didn't like. Nothing he had done to her she didn't love. She liked the way he felt, and apparently she liked the way he tasted, too.

She parted her lips slowly, worked them over the head, then swallowed down as much of him as she could. The accompanying sound he made hollowed out her stomach, made her feel weak and powerful at the same time.

His body was such an amazing thing. So strong, like it had been carved straight from the mountain. Yet it wasn't in any way cold or unmovable; it was hot. His body had changed hers. Yes, he'd taken her virginity, but he had also taught her to feel pleasure she hadn't realized she had the capacity to feel.

Such power in his body, and yet, right now, it trembled beneath her touch. The whisper-soft touch of her lips possessed the power to rock him, to make him shake. To make him shatter.

Right now, desire was enough. She didn't need skill. She didn't need experience. And she felt completely confident in that.

She slipped her tongue over his length as she took him in deep, and he bucked his hips lightly, touching the back of her throat. Her throat contracted and he jerked back.

"Sorry," he said, his voice strained.

"No," she said, gripping him with one hand and bringing her lips back against him. "Don't apologize. I like it."

"You're inexperienced."

She nodded slowly, then traced him with the tip of her tongue. "Yes," she agreed, "I am. I've never done this for any other man. I've never even thought about it before." His hips jerked again, and she realized he liked this. That he—however much he tried to pretend he didn't—liked that her desire was all for him.

"I think you might be corrupting me," she said, keeping her eyes wide as she took him back into her mouth.

He grunted, fisting his hands in her hair, but he didn't pull her away again.

The muscles in his thighs twitched beneath her fingertips, and he seemed to grow larger, harder in her mouth. She increased the suction, increased the friction, used her hands as well as her mouth to drive him as crazy as she possibly could.

There was no plan. There was no skill. There was just the need to make him even half as mindless as he'd made her over the past couple days.

He had changed her. He had taken her from innocence…to this. She would be marked by him forever. He would always be her first. But society didn't have a term for a person's experience after virginity. So she didn't have a label for the impact she wanted to make on him.

Jonathan hadn't been a virgin for a very long time, she suspected. And she probably wasn't particularly special as a sexual partner.

So she had to try to make herself special.

She had no tricks to make this the best experience he'd ever had. She had only herself. And so she gave it to him. All of her. Everything.

"Hayley," he said, his voice rough, ragged. "You better stop."

She didn't. She ignored him. She had a feeling he was close; she recognized the signs now. She had watched him reach the point of pleasure enough times that she had a fair idea of what it looked like. Of what it felt like. His whole body tensing, his movements becoming less controlled.

She squeezed the base of him tightly, pulling him in deeper, and then he shattered. And she swallowed down every last shudder of need that racked his big body.

In the aftermath, she was dazed, her heart pounding hard, her entire body buzzing. She looked up at him from her position on the floor, and he looked down at her, his dark eyes blazing with…anger, maybe? Passion? A kind of sharp, raw need she hadn't ever seen before.

"You're going to pay for that," he said.

"Oh," she returned, "I hope so."

He swept her up, crushed her against his chest. "You have to put it on my list first," she said.

Then he brought his mouth down to hers, and whatever she'd intended to write down was forgotten until morning.

Ten

Sometime on Sunday afternoon Hayley had gone home. Because, she had insisted, she wasn't able to work in either his T-shirt or the dress she had worn to the bar on Friday.

He hadn't agreed, but he had been relieved to have the reprieve. He didn't feel comfortable sharing the bed with her while he slept. Which had meant sleeping on the couch in the office after she drifted off.

He just… He didn't sleep with women. He didn't see the point in inviting that kind of intimacy. Having her spend the night in his bed was bad enough. But he hadn't wanted to send her home, either. He didn't want to think about why. Maybe it was because she expected to stay, because of her general inexperience.

Which made him think of the moment she had taken him into her mouth, letting him know he was the first man she had ever considered doing that for. Just the thought of it made his eyes roll back in his head.

Now, it was late Monday afternoon and she had been slowly driving him crazy with the prim little outfit she had come back to work in, as though he didn't know what she looked like underneath it.

Who knew he'd like a good girl who gave head like a dream.

She had also insisted that they stay professional during work hours, and it was making it hard for him to concentrate. Of course, it was always hard for him to concentrate on office work. In general, he hated it.

Though bringing Hayley into the office certainly made it easier to bear.

Except for the part where it was torture.

He stood up from his chair and stretched slowly, trying to work the tension out of his body. But he had a feeling that until he was buried inside Hayley's body again, tension was just going to be the state of things.

"Oh," Hayley said, "Joshua Grayson just emailed and said he needs you to go by the county office and sign a form. And no, it can't be faxed."

For the first time in his life, Johathan was relieved to encounter bureaucracy. He needed to get out of this space. He needed to get his head on straight.

"Great," he said.

"Maybe I should go with you," she said. "I've never been down to the building and planning office, and you might need me to run errands in the future."

He gritted his teeth. "Yeah, probably."

"I'll drive my own car." She stood, grabbing her purse off the desk. "Because by the time we're done it will be time for me to get off."

He ground his teeth together even harder, because he couldn't ignore her double entendre even though he knew it had been accidental. And because, in addition to the double meaning, it was clear she intended to stay in town tonight and not at his place.

He should probably be grateful she wasn't being clingy. He didn't like to encourage women to get too attached to him, not at all.

"Great idea," he said.

But he didn't think it was a great idea, and he grumbled the entire way to town in the solitude of his pickup truck, not missing the irony that he had been wanting alone time, and was now getting it, and was upset about it.

The errand really did take only a few minutes, and afterward it still wasn't quite time for Hayley to clock out.

"Do you want to grab something to eat?" he asked,

though he had no earthly idea why. He should get something for himself and go home, deal with that tension he had been pondering earlier.

She looked back and forth, clearly edgy. "In town?"

"Yes," he returned, "in town."

"Oh. I don't… I guess so."

"Calm down," he said. "I'm not asking you to Beaches. Let's just stop by the Crab Shanty."

She looked visibly relieved, and again he couldn't quantify why that annoyed him.

He knew they shouldn't be seen together in town. He had a feeling she also liked the casual nature of the restaurant. It was much more likely to look like a boss and employee grabbing something to eat than it was to look like a date.

They walked from where they had parked a few streets over, and paused at the crosswalk. They waited for one car to crawl by, clearly not interested in heeding the law that said pedestrians had the right-of-way. Then Jonathan charged ahead of her across the street and up to the faded yellow building. A small line was already forming outside the order window, and he noticed that Hayley took pains to stand slightly behind him.

When it was their turn to order, he decided he wasn't having any of her missish circumspection. They shouldn't be seen together as anything more than a boss and an assistant.

But right now, hell if he cared. "Two orders of fish and chips, the halibut. Two beers and a Diet Coke."

He pulled his wallet out and paid before Hayley could protest, then he grabbed the plastic number from the window, and the two of them walked over to a picnic table positioned outside the ramshackle building. There was no indoor seating, which could be a little bracing on windy days, and there weren't very many days that didn't have wind on the Oregon coast.

Jonathan set the number on the wooden table, then sat down heavily, looking up at the blue-and-white-striped umbrella wiggling in the breeze.

"Two beers?"

"One of them is for you," he said, his words verging on a growl.

"I'm not going to drink a beer." She looked sideways. "At least not here."

"Yeah, right out here on Main Street in front of God and everybody? You're a lot braver in my bedroom."

He was goading her, but he didn't much care. He was… Well dammit, it pissed him off. To see how ashamed she was to be with him. How desperate she was to hide it. Even if he understood it, it was like a branding iron straight to the gut.

"You can't say that so loud," she hissed, leaning forward, grabbing the plastic number and pulling it to her chest. "What if people heard you?"

"I thought you were reinventing yourself, Hayley Thompson."

"Not for the benefit of…the town. It's about me."

"It's going to be about you not getting dinner if you keep hiding our number." He snatched the plastic triangle from her hands.

She let out a heavy sigh and leaned back, crossing her arms. "Well, the extra beer is for you. Put it in your pocket."

"You can put it in your own pocket. Drink it back at your place."

"No, thanks."

"Don't you want to tick that box on your list? We ticked off some pretty interesting ones last night."

Her face turned scarlet. "You're being obnoxious, Jonathan."

"I've been obnoxious from day one. You just found it easy to ignore when I had my hand in your pants."

Her mouth dropped open, then she snapped it shut again. Their conversation was cut off when their food was placed in front of them.

She dragged the white cardboard box toward her and opened it, removing the container of coleslaw and setting it to the side before grabbing a french fry and biting into it fiercely. Her annoyance was clearly telegraphed by the ferocity with which she ate each bite of food. And the determination that went into her looking at anything and everything around them except for him.

"Enjoying the view?" he asked after a moment.

"The ocean is very pretty," she snapped.

"And you don't see it every day?"

"I never tire of the majesty of nature."

His lips twitched, in spite of his irritation. "Of course not."

The wind whipped up, blowing a strand of dark hair into Hayley's face. Reflexively, he reached across the table and pushed it out of her eyes. She jerked back, her lips going slack, her expression shocked.

"You're my boss," she said, her voice low. "As far as everyone is concerned."

"Well," he said, "I'm your lover. As far as I'm concerned."

"Stop."

"I thought you wanted new experiences? I thought you were tired of hiding? And here you are, hiding."

"I don't want to…perform," she said. "My new experiences are for me. Not for everyone else's consumption. That's why I'm leaving. So I can…do things without an audience."

"You want your dirty secrets, is that it? You want me to be your dirty secret."

"It's five o'clock," she said, her tone stiff. "I'm going to go home now."

She collected her food, and left the beer, standing up in a huff and taking off down the street in the opposite direction from where they had parked.

"Where are you going?"

"Home," she said sharply.

He gathered up the rest of the food and stomped after her. "You parked the other way."

"I'll get it in the morning."

"Then you better leave your house early. Unless this is you tendering your resignation."

"I'm not quitting," she said, the color heightening in her face. "I'm just… I'm irritated with you."

She turned away from him, continuing to walk quickly down the street. He took two strides and caught up with her. "I see that." He kept pace with her, but she seemed bound and determined not to look at him. "Would you care to share why?"

"Not even a little bit."

"So you're insisting that you're my employee, and that you want to be treated like my employee in public. But that clearly excludes when you decide to run off having a temper tantrum."

She whirled around then, stopping in her tracks. "Why are you acting like this? You've been…much more careful than this up till now." She sniffed. "Out of deference to my innocence?"

"What innocence, baby? Because I took that." He smiled, knowing he was getting to her. That he was making her feel as bad as he did. "Pretty damn thoroughly."

"I can't do this with you. Not here." She paused at the street corner and looked both ways before hurrying across the two-lane road. He followed suit. She walked down the sidewalk, passed the coffeehouse, which was closing up for the day, then rounded the side of the brick building and headed toward the back.

"Is this where you live?" he asked.

"Maybe," she returned, sounding almost comically stubborn. Except he didn't feel like much was funny about this situation.

"Here in the alley?" he asked, waving his hand around the mostly vacant space.

"Yes. In the Dumpster with the mice. It's not so bad. I shredded up a bunch of newspaper and made a little bed."

"I suspect this is the real reason you've been spending the night at my place, then."

She scowled. "If you want to fight with me, come upstairs."

He didn't want to fight with her. He wanted to grab her, pull her into his arms and kiss her. He wanted to stop talking. Wanted to act logical instead of being wounded by something he knew he should want to avoid.

It didn't benefit him to have anyone in town know what he was doing with Hayley. He should want to hide it as badly as she did.

But the idea that she was enjoying his body, enjoying slumming it with him in the sheets, and was damned ashamed of him in the streets burned like hell.

But he followed her through the back door to a little hallway that contained two other doors. She unlocked one of them and held it open for him. Then she gestured to the narrow staircase. "Come on."

"Who's the boss around here?"

"I'm off the clock," she said.

He shrugged, then walked up the stairs and into an open-plan living room with exposed beams and brick. It was a much bigger space than he had expected it to be, though it was also mostly empty. As if she had only half committed to living there.

But then, he supposed, her plan *was* to travel the world.

"Nice place," he said.

"Yeah," she said. "Cassie gave me a deal."

"Nice of her."

"Some people are nice, Jonathan."

"Meaning I'm not?" he asked.

She nodded in response, her mouth firmly sealed, her chin jutting out stubbornly.

"Right. Because I bought you fish and french fries and beer. And I give you really great orgasms. I'm a monster."

"I don't know what game you're playing," she said, suddenly looking much less stubborn and a little more wobbly. And that made him feel something close to guilty. "What's the point in blurring the lines while we walk through town? We both know this isn't a relationship. It's…it's boxes being ticked on a list."

"Sure. But why does it matter if people in town know you're doing that?"

"You know why it matters. Don't play like you don't understand. You do. I know you do. You know who I am, and you know that I feel like I'm under a microscope. I shared all of that with you. Don't act surprised by it now."

"Well," he said, opting for honesty even though he knew it was a damned bad idea. "Maybe I don't like being your dirty secret."

"It's not about you. Any guy that I was… Anyone that I was…doing this with. It would be a secret. It has to be."

"Why?"

"Because!" she exploded. "Because everyone will be…disappointed."

"Honey," he said, "I don't think people spend half as much time thinking about you as you think they do."

"No," she said. "They do. You know Ace. He's the pastor's son. He ran away from home, he got married, he got divorced. Then he came back and opened a bar. My parents…they're great. They really are. But they had a lot of backlash over that. People saying that the Bible itself says if you train up a child the way he should go, he's not going to depart from it. Well, he departed from it, at least as far as a lot of the congregants were concerned. People actually left the church." She sucked in a sharp breath, then let it out slowly. "I wanted to do better than that for them. It was important. For me to be…the good one."

Caring about what people thought was a strange concept. Appearances had never mattered to Jonathan. For him, it had always been about actions. What the hell did Rebecca care if he had been good? All she cared about was being taken care of. He couldn't imagine being bound by rules like that.

For the first time, he wondered if there wasn't some kind of freedom in no one having a single good expectation of you.

"But you don't like being the good one. At least, not by these standards."

Her eyes glittered with tears now. She shook her head. "I don't know. I just… I don't know. I'm afraid. Afraid of what people will think. Afraid of what my parents will think. Afraid of them being disappointed. And hurt. They've always put a lot of stock in me being what Ace wasn't. They love Ace, don't get me wrong. It's just…"

"He made things hard for them."

Hayley nodded, looking miserable. "Yes. He did. And I don't want to do that. Only…only, I was the good one and he still ended up with the kind of life I want."

"Is that all?" Jonathan asked. "Or are you afraid

of who you might be if you don't have all those rules to follow?"

A flash of fear showed in her eyes, and he felt a little guilty about putting it there. Not guilty enough to take it back. Not guilty enough to stay away from her. Not guilty enough to keep his hands to himself. He reached out, cupping her cheek, then wrapped his arm around her waist and drew her toward him. "Does it scare you? Who you might be if no one told you what to do? I don't care about the rules, Hayley. You can be whoever you want with me. Say whatever you want. Drink whatever you want. Do whatever you want."

"I don't know," she said, wiggling against him, trying to pull away. "I don't know what I want."

"I think you do. I just think you wish you wanted something else." He brushed his thumb over her cheekbone. "I think you like having rules because it keeps you from going after what scares you."

He ignored the strange reverberation those words set off inside him. The chain reaction that seemed to burst all the way down his spine.

Recognition.

Truth.

Yeah, he ignored all that, and he dipped his head, claiming her mouth with his own.

Suddenly, it seemed imperative that he have her here. In her apartment. That he wreck this place with his desire for her. That he have her on every surface, against every wall, so that whenever she walked in, whenever she looked around, he was what she thought of. So that she couldn't escape this. So that she couldn't escape him.

"You think you know me now?" she asked, her eyes squinting with challenge. Clearly, she wasn't going to back down without a fight. And that was one of the things he liked about her. For all that she was an innocent church secretary, she had spirit. She had the kind of steel backbone that he admired, that he respected. The kind of strength that could get you through anything. But there was a softness to her as well, and that was something more foreign to him. Something he had never been exposed to, had never really been allowed to have.

"Yeah," he said, tightening his hold and drawing her against his body. "I know you. I know what you look like naked. I know every inch of your skin. How it feels, how it tastes. I know you better than anybody does, baby. You can tell yourself that's not true. You can say that this, what we have, is the crazy thing. That it's a break from your real life. That it's some detour you don't want anyone in town to know you're taking. But I know the truth. And I think somewhere deep down you know it, too. This isn't the break. All that other stuff…prim, proper church girl. That's what isn't real." He cupped her face, smoothing his thumbs over her cheeks. "You're fire, honey, and together we are an explosion."

He kissed her then, proving his point. She tasted like anger, like need, and he was of a mind to consume both. Whatever was on offer. Whatever she would give him.

He was beyond himself. He had never wanted a woman like this before. He had never wanted anything quite like this before. Not money, not security, not his damned house on the hill.

All that want, all that need, paled in comparison to what he felt for Hayley Thompson. The innocent little miss who should have bored him to tears by now, had him aching, panting and begging for more.

He was so hard he was in physical pain.

And when she finally capitulated, when she gave herself over to the kiss, soft fingertips skimming his shoulders, down his back, all the way to his ass, he groaned in appreciation.

There was something extra dirty about Hayley exploring his body. About her wanting him the way she did, because she had never wanted another man like she wanted him. By her own admission. And she had never had a man the way she'd had him, which was an admission she didn't have to make.

He gripped her hips, then slipped his hands down her thighs, grabbing them and pulling her up, urging her legs around his waist. Then he propelled them both across the living room, down onto the couch. He covered her, pressing his hardness against the soft, sweet apex of her thighs. She gasped as he rolled his hips forward.

"Not so ashamed of this now, are you?" He growled, pressing a kiss to her neck, then to her collarbone, then to the edge of her T-shirt.

"I'm not ashamed," she said, gasping for air.

"You could've fooled me, princess."

"It's not about you." She sifted her fingers through his hair. "I'm not ashamed of you."

"Not ashamed of your dirty, wrong-side-of-the-tracks boyfriend?"

Her eyes flashed with hurt and then fascination. "I've never thought of you that way. I never... *Boyfriend?*"

Something burned hot in his chest. "Lover. Whatever."

"I'm not ashamed of you," she reiterated. "Nothing about you. You're so beautiful. If anything, you ought to be ashamed of me. I'm not pretty. Not like you. And I don't even know what I'm doing. I just know what I want. I want you. And I'm afraid for anybody to know the truth. I'm so scared. The only time I'm not scared is when you're holding me."

He didn't want to talk anymore. He consumed her mouth, tasting her deeply, ramping up the arousal between them with each sweet stroke of his tongue across hers. With each deep taste of the sweet flavor that could only ever be Hayley.

He gripped the hem of her top, yanking it over

her head, making quick work of her bra. Exposing small, perfect breasts to his inspection. She was pale. All over. Ivory skin, coral-pink nipples. He loved the look of her. Loved the feel of her. Loved so many things about her that it was tempting to just go ahead and say he loved *her*.

That thought swam thick and dizzy in his head. He could barely grab hold of it, didn't want to. So he shoved it to the side. He wasn't going to claim that. Hell no.

He didn't love people. He loved *things*.

He could love her tits, and he could love her skin, could love the way it felt to slide inside her, slick and tight. But he sure as hell couldn't love *her*.

He bent his head, taking one hardened nipple into his mouth, sucking hard, relishing the horse sound of pleasure on her lips as he did so. Then he kissed his way down her stomach, to the edge of her pants, pulling them down her thighs, leaving her bare and open.

He pressed his hand between her legs, slicked his thumb over her, teased her entrance with one finger. She began to whimper, rolling her hips under him, arching them to meet him, and he watched. Watched as she took one finger inside, then another.

He damn well watched himself corrupt her, and he let himself enjoy it. Because he was sick, because he was broken, but at least it wasn't a surprise.

Everyone in his life was familiar with it.

His father had tried to beat it out of him. His mother had run from it.

Only Rebecca had ever stayed, and it was partly because she didn't know any better.

Hayley didn't know any better, either, come to that. Not really. Not when it came to men. Not when it came to sex. She was blinded by what he could make her body feel, so she had an easy enough time ignoring the rest. But that wouldn't last forever.

Fair enough, since they wouldn't last forever, anyway. They both knew it. So there was no point in worrying about it. Not really.

Instead, he would embrace this, embrace the rush. Embrace the hollowed out feeling in his gut that bordered on sickness. The tension in his body that verged on pain. The need that rendered him hard as iron and hot as fire.

"Come for me," he commanded, his voice hoarse. All other words, all other thoughts were lost to him. All he could do was watch her writhing beneath his touch, so hot, so wet for him, arching her hips and taking his fingers in deeper.

"Not yet," she gasped, emitting little broken sounds.

"Yes," he said. "You will. You're going to come for me now, Hayley, because I told you to. Your body is mine. You're mine." He slid his thumb over the delicate bundle of nerves there.

And then he felt her shatter beneath his touch. Felt her internal muscles pulse around his knuckles.

He reached into his back pocket, took out his wallet and found a condom quickly. He tore it open, then wrenched free his belt buckle and took down the zipper. He pushed his jeans partway down his hips, rolled the condom on his hard length and thrust inside her, all the way to the hilt. She was wet and ready for him, and he had to grit his teeth to keep from embarrassing himself, to keep it from being over before it had begun.

She gasped as he filled her, and then grabbed his ass when he retreated. Her fingernails dug into his skin, and he relished the pain this petite little thing could inflict on him. Of course, it was nothing compared to the pain he felt from his arousal. From the great, burning need inside him.

No, nothing compared to that. Nothing at all.

He adjusted their positions, dragging her sideways on the couch, bringing her hips to the edge of the cushion, going down on his knees to the hardwood floor.

He knelt there, gripping her hips and pulling her tightly against him, urging her to wrap her legs around him. The floor bit into his knees, but he didn't care. All he cared about was having her, taking her, claiming her. He gripped her tightly, his blunt fingertips digging into her flesh.

He wondered if he would leave a mark. He hoped he might.

Hoped that she would see for days to come where

he had held her. Even if she wouldn't hold his hand in public, she would remember when he'd held her hips in private, when he'd driven himself deep inside her, clinging to her like she might be the source of all life.

Yeah, she would remember that. She would remember this.

He watched as a deep red flush spread over her skin, covering her breasts, creeping up her neck. She was on the verge of another orgasm. He loved that. Another thing he was allowed to love.

Loved watching her lose control. Loved watching her so close to giving it up for him again, completely. Utterly. He was going to ruin her for any other man. That was his vow, there and then, on the floor of her apartment, with a ragged splinter digging into his knee through the fabric of his jeans. She was never going to fuck anyone else without thinking of him. Without wanting him. Without wishing it were him.

She would go to Paris, and some guy would do her with a view of the Eiffel tower in the background. And she would wish she were here, counting the familiar beams on her ceiling.

And when she came home for a visit and she passed him on the street, she would shiver with a longing that she would never quite get rid of.

So many people in his life had left him. As far as he'd known, they had done it without a backward glance. But Hayley would never forget him. He would make sure of it. Damn sure.

His own arousal ratcheted up to impossible proportions. He was made entirely of his need for her. Of his need for release. And he forgot what he was trying to do. Forgot that this was about her. That this was about making her tremble, making her shake. Because he was trembling. He was shaking.

He was afraid he might be the one who was indelibly marked by all this.

He was the one who wouldn't be able to forget. The one who would never be with anyone else without thinking of her. No matter how skilled the woman was who might come after her, it would never be the same as the sweet, genuine urging of Hayley's hips against his. It would never be quite like the tight, wet clasp of her body.

He had been entirely reshaped, remade, to fit inside her, and no one else would do.

That thought ignited in his stomach, overtook him completely, lit him on fire.

When he came, it was with her name on his lips, with a strange satisfaction washing through him that left him only hungrier in the end, emptier. Because this was ending, and he knew it.

She wasn't going to work for him forever. She wasn't going to stay in Copper Ridge. She might hold on to him in secret, but in public, she would never touch him.

And as time passed, she would let go of him by inches, walking off to the life of freedom she was so desperate for.

Walking off like everyone else.

Right now, she was looking up at him, a mixture of wonder and deep emotion visible in her blue eyes. She reached up, stroking his face. Some of his hair had been tugged from the leather strap, and she brushed the strands out of his eyes.

It was weird how that hit him. How it touched him. After all the overtly sexual ways she'd put her hands on him, why that sweet gesture impacted him low and deep.

"Stay with me," she said, her voice soft. "The night. In my bed."

That hit even harder.

He had never slept with her. He didn't sleep with women. But that was all about to change. He was going to sleep with her because he wanted to. Because he didn't want to release his hold on her for one moment, not while he still had her.

"Okay," he said.

Then, still buried deep inside her, he picked her up from the couch, brought them both to a standing position and started walking toward the door at the back of the room. "Bedroom is this way?"

"How did you know?"

"Important things, I know. Where the bedroom

is." He kissed her lips. "How to make you scream my name. That I know."

"Care to make me scream it a few more times?"

"The neighbors might hear."

It was a joke, but he could still see her hesitation. "That's okay," she said slowly.

And even though he was reasonably confident that was a lie, he carried her into her bedroom and lay down on the bed with her.

It didn't matter if it was a lie. Because they had all night to live in it. And that was good enough for him.

Eleven

When he woke up the next morning he was disoriented. He was lying in a bed that was too small for his large frame, and he had a woman wrapped around him. Of course, he knew immediately which woman it was. It couldn't be anyone else. Even in the fog of sleep, he wasn't confused about Hayley's identity.

She smelled like sunshine and wildflowers. Or maybe she just smelled like soap and skin and only reminded him of sunshine and wildflowers, because they were innocent things. New things. The kinds of things that could never be corrupted by the world around them.

The kinds of things not even he could wreck.

She was that kind of beautiful.

But the other reason he was certain it was Hayley was that there was no other woman he would have fallen asleep with. It was far too intimate a thing, sharing a bed with someone when you weren't angling for an orgasm. He had never seen the point of it. It was basically the same as sharing a toothbrush, and he wasn't interested in that, either.

He looked at Hayley, curled up at his side, her brown hair falling across her face, her soft lips parted, her breathing easy and deep. The feeling carved out in his chest was a strange one.

Hell, lying there in the early morning, sharing a toothbrush with Hayley didn't even seem so insane.

He sat up, shaking off the last cobwebs of sleep and extricating himself from Hayley's hold. He groaned when her fingertips brushed the lower part of his stomach, grazing his insistent morning erection. He had half a mind to wake her up the best way he knew how.

But the longer the realization of what had happened last night sat with him, the more eager he was to put some distance between them.

He could get some coffee, get his head on straight and come back fully clothed. Then maybe the two of them could prepare for the workday.

He needed to compartmentalize. He had forgotten that yesterday. He had let himself get annoyed about something that never should have bothered him. Had allowed old hurts to sink in when he shouldn't give a damn whether or not Hayley wanted to hold his hand when they walked down the street. She wasn't his girlfriend. And all the words that had passed between them in the apartment, all the anger that had been rattling around inside him, seemed strange now. Like it had all happened to somebody else. The morning had brought clarity, and it was much needed.

He hunted around the room, collecting his clothes and tugging them on quickly, then he walked over to the window, drew back the curtains and tried to get a sense of what time it was. She didn't have a clock in her room. He wondered if she just looked at her phone.

The sky was pink, so it had to be nearing six. He really needed to get home and take care of the horses. He didn't want to mess up their routine. But he would come back. Or maybe Hayley would just come to his place on time.

Then he cursed, realizing he had left his car at the other end of Main Street. He walked back to the living room, pulled on his boots and headed out the door, down the stairs. His vision was blurry, and he was in desperate need of caffeine. There were two doors in the hallway, and he reached for the one closest to him.

And nearly ran right into Cassie Caldwell as he walked into The Grind.

The morning sounds of the coffee shop filled his ears, the intense smell of the roast assaulting him in the best way.

But Cassie was staring at him, wide-eyed, as were the ten people sitting inside the dining room. One of whom happened to be Pastor John Thompson.

Jonathan froze, mumbled something about coming in through the back door, and then walked up to the counter. He was going to act like there was nothing remarkable about where he had just come from. Was going to do his very best to look like there was nothing at all strange about him coming through what he now realized was a private entrance used only by the tenant upstairs. It didn't escape his notice that the pastor was eyeballing him closely. And so was Cassie. Really, so was everybody. Damn small town.

Now, he could see why Hayley had been so vigilant yesterday.

If only he could go back and be vigilant in his door choice.

"Black coffee," he said, "two shots of espresso."

Cassie's gaze turned hard. "I know."

"I came through the wrong door," he said.

She walked over to the espresso machine, wrapped a damp cloth around the wand that steamed the milk and twisted it, a puff of steam coming out as she jerked the cloth up and down roughly, her eyes never leaving his. "Uh-huh."

"I did."

"And it's just a coincidence that my tenant happens to live upstairs. My tenant who works for you." She said that part softly, and he was sure nobody else in the room heard it.

"That's right," he said. "Just a coincidence."

Suddenly, the door to the coffee shop opened again, and Hayley appeared, wearing a T-shirt and jeans, her hair wild, like she had just rolled out of bed.

Her eyes widened when she saw her father. Then she looked over at the counter and her eyes widened even further when she saw Jonathan.

"Good morning," he said, his voice hard. "Fancy meeting you here before work."

"Yes," she said. "I'm just gonna go get ready."

She turned around and walked back out of the coffee shop, as quickly as she had come in. So much for being casual. If he hadn't already given it away, he was pretty sure Hayley's scampering had.

"You were saying?" Cassie said, her tone brittle.

"I'm sorry," he said, leaning in. "Is she your sister?"

"No."

"Best friend?"

"No."

"Is she your daughter? Because I have a feeling I'm about to catch hell from the reverend here in a few minutes, but I'm not really sure why I'm catching it from you."

"Because I know her. I know all about you. I am friends with your sister, and I know enough through her."

"Undoubtedly all about my great personal sacrifice and sparkling personality," he said.

Cassie's expression softened. "Rebecca loves you. But she's also realistic about the fact that you aren't a love-and-commitment kind of guy. Also, I do believe Ms. Hayley Thompson is younger than your sister."

"And last I checked, I wasn't committing any crimes. I will just take the coffee. You can keep the lecture."

He was not going to get chased out of the coffee shop, no matter how many people looked at him. No matter how much Cassie lectured him.

He was not the poor kid he'd once been. He was more than just a boy who had been abandoned by both parents. He was a damned boon to the town. His business brought in good money. *He* brought in good money. He wasn't going to be treated like dirt beneath anybody's shoe.

Maybe Hayley was too good for him, but she was sleeping with him. She wanted him. So it wasn't really up to anybody to say that she shouldn't.

When he turned around after Cassie gave him his coffee, the pastor stood up at his table and began to make his way over to Jonathan.

"Hello. Jonathan, right?" the older man said, his voice shot through with the same kind of steel that

Jonathan often heard in Hayley's voice. Clearly, she got her strength from her father. It was also clear to Jonathan that he was not being spoken to by a pastor at the moment. But by a fairly angry dad.

"Pastor John," Jonathan said by way of greeting.

"Why don't you join me for a cup of coffee?"

Not exactly the words Jonathan had expected, all things considered. He could sense the tension in the room, sense the tension coming off Hayley's father.

People were doing their very best to watch, without appearing to do so. Any hope Jonathan had retained that they were oblivious to what it meant that he had come down from the upstairs apartment was dashed by just how fascinated they all were. And by the steady intent on Pastor John's face.

If the old man wanted to sit him down and humiliate him in front of the town, wanted to talk about how Jonathan wasn't fit to lick the dust off Hayley's boots, Jonathan wouldn't be surprised. Hell, he welcomed it. It was true, after all.

"I think I will," Jonathan said, following the other man back to his table.

He took a seat, his hand curled tightly around his coffee cup.

"I don't think we've ever formally met," John said, leaning back in his chair.

"No," Jonathan said, "we wouldn't have. I don't recall darkening the door of the church in my lifetime. Unless it was to repair something."

Let him know just what kind of man Jonathan was. That's where this was headed, anyway. Jonathan had never met a woman's parents before. He had never been in a relationship that was serious enough to do so. And this wasn't serious, either. But because of this damn small town and Hayley's role in it, he was being forced into a position he had never wanted to be in.

"I see," the pastor said. "Hayley has been working for you for the past couple of weeks, I believe."

He was cutting right to the chase now. To Jonathan's connection to Hayley, which was undeniable. "Yes."

"I've been very protective of Hayley. Possibly overprotective. But when my son, Ace, went out on his own, he didn't find much but heartbreak. I transferred some of my fear of that happening again onto Hayley, to an unfair degree. So I kept her close. I encouraged her to keep working at the church. To live at home for as long as possible. You have a sister, don't you?"

Damn this man and his ironclad memory for detail. "I didn't think it was Christian to gossip. But I can see that you've certainly heard your share about me."

"I do know a little something about you, yes. My son is married to one of Nathan West's children, as I'm sure you know. And your sister has a connection to that family, as well."

Jonathan gritted his teeth. "Yes. My sister is with Gage. Though only God knows why. Maybe you could ask Him."

"Matters of the heart are rarely straightforward. Whether it's in the case of romantic love, or the love you feel for your children, or your sister. It's a big emotion. And it is scary at times. Not always the most rational. What you feel about Rebecca being with Gage I suppose is similar to the concerns I have about Hayley."

"That she's with a bastard who doesn't deserve her?"

The pastor didn't even flinch. "That she's involved deeply enough that she could be hurt. And if we're going to speak plainly, I suppose the question I could ask you is whether or not you would think any man was good enough for Rebecca, or if you would be concerned—no matter who it was—that he wouldn't handle her with the care you would want."

Jonathan didn't have much to say about that. Only because he was trying to be angry. Trying to take offense at the fact that the older man was questioning him. Trying to connect this conversation to what he knew to be true—everybody looked at him and saw someone who wasn't worthy. He certainly didn't deserve kindness from this man, not at all. Didn't deserve for him to sit here and try to forge some kind of connection.

Jonathan had taken advantage of Hayley. Regardless of her level of experience, she was his employee. Even if she had been with a hundred men, what he had done would be problematic. But, as far as he was concerned, the problem was compounded by the fact that Hayley had been innocent.

So he waited. He waited for that hammer to fall. For the accusations to fly.

But they didn't come. So he figured he might try to create a few.

"I'm sure there's a certain type of man you would prefer your daughter be with. But it's definitely not the guy with the bad reputation you'd want stumbling out of her apartment early in the morning."

John nodded slowly, and Jonathan thought—with a certain amount of triumph—that he saw anger flicker briefly in the older man's eyes.

"I told you already that I feel very protective of her," Pastor John said. "But I wonder if, by protecting her as much as I did, I shielded her too effectively from the reality of life. I don't want her to get hurt." He let out a long, slow breath. "But that is not within my control."

"Is this the part where you ask me about my intentions toward your daughter? Because I highly doubt we're ever going to sit around a dinner table and try to make small talk. This isn't that sort of thing." With those words, Jonathan effectively told Hayley's father that all he was doing was fooling around with her. And that wasn't strictly true. Also, he hated himself a little bit for pretending it was.

For saying that sort of thing to her father when he knew it would embarrass her.

But in a way, it would be a mercy. She cared what people in town thought about her. She cared about her father's opinion. And this conversation would make it so much easier for her to let Jonathan go when the time came.

She was always going to let you go. She has traveling to do, places to see. You were her dirty detour along the way. You're the one who needs distance. You're the one who needs to find a way to make it easier.

He ignored that voice, ignored the tightening in his chest.

"Why isn't it that sort of thing?" The question, issued from Hayley's father, his tone firm but steady, reached something deep inside Jonathan, twisted it, cracked it.

It couldn't be anything more than temporary. Because of him. Because of what he was. Who he was. That should be obvious. It would have been even more obvious if Pastor John had simply sat down and started hurling recriminations. About how Jonathan was beneath the man's pure, innocent daughter. About why a formerly impoverished man from the wrong side of the tracks could never be good enough for a woman like her.

It didn't matter that he had money now. He was the same person he had been born to be. The same boy who had been beaten by his father, abandoned by his mother. All that was still in him. And no custom home, no amount of money in his bank account, was ever going to fix it.

If John Thompson wouldn't look at him and see that, if he wouldn't shout it from across a crowded coffee shop so the whole town would hear, then Jonathan was going to have to make it clear.

"Because it's not something I do," he returned, his voice hard. "I'm in for temporary. That's all I've got."

"Well," John said, "that's a pretty neat lie you've been telling yourself, son. But the fact of the matter is, it's only the most you're willing to give, not the most you have the ability to give."

"And you're saying you want me to dig down deep and find it inside myself to be with your daughter forever? Something tells me that probably wouldn't be an ideal situation as far as you're concerned."

"That's between you and Hayley. I have my own personal feelings about it, to be sure. No father wants to believe that his daughter is being used. But if I believe that, then it means I don't see anything good in you, and that isn't true. Everybody knows how you took care of your sister. Whatever you think the people in this town believe about you, they do know that. I can't say you haven't been mistreated by the people here, and it grieves me to think about it."

He shook his head, and Jonathan was forced to believe the older man was being genuine. He didn't quite know what to do with that fact, but he saw the same honesty shining from John that he often saw in Hayley's eyes. An emotional honesty Jonathan had limited experience with.

The older man continued. "You think you don't have the capacity for love? When you've already mentioned your concern for Rebecca a couple of times in this conversation? When the past decade and a half of your life was devoted to caring for her? It's no secret how hard you've worked. I may never have formally met you until this moment, but I know about you, Jonathan Bear, and what I know isn't the reputation you seem to think you have."

"Well, regardless of my reputation, you should be concerned about Hayley's. When I came through that door this morning, it was unintentional. But it's important to Hayley that nobody realizes what's happening between us. So the longer I sit here talking to you, the more risk there is of exposing her to unnecessary chatter. And that's not what I want. So," he said, "out of respect for keeping it a secret, like Hayley wants—"

"That's not what I want."

Twelve

Hayley was shaking. She had been shaking from the moment she had walked into The Grind and seen Jonathan there, with her father in the background.

Somehow, she had known—just known—that everyone in the room was putting two and two together and coming up with sex.

And she also knew she had definitely made it worse by running away. If she had sauntered in and acted surprised to see Jonathan there, she might have made people think it really was coincidental that the two of them were both in the coffeehouse early in the morning, coming through the same private door. For reasons that had nothing to do with him spending the night upstairs with her.

But she had spent the past five minutes pacing around upstairs, waiting for her breath to normalize, waiting for her heart to stop beating so hard. Neither thing had happened.

Then she had cautiously crept back downstairs and come in to see her father sitting at the table with Jonathan. Fortunately, Jonathan hadn't looked like he'd been punched in the face. But the conversation had definitely seemed tense.

And standing there, looking at what had been her worst nightmare not so long ago, she realized that it just…wasn't. She'd never been ashamed of Jonathan. He was…the most determined, hardworking, wonderful man she had ever known. He had spent his life raising his sister. He had experienced a childhood where he had known nothing but abandonment and abuse, and he had turned around and given love to his sister, unconditionally and tirelessly.

And, yeah, maybe it wasn't ideal to announce her physical affair with him at the coffee shop, all things considered, but…whatever she had expected to feel… She didn't.

So, it had been the easiest thing in the world to walk over to their table and say that she really didn't need to keep their relationship a secret. Of course, now both Jonathan and her father were looking at her like she had grown a second head.

When she didn't get a response from either of them, she repeated, "That's not what I want."

"Hayley," Jonathan said, his tone firm. "You don't know what you're saying."

"Oh, please," she returned. "Jonathan, that tone wouldn't work on me in private, and it's not going to work on me here, either."

She took a deep breath, shifting her weight from foot to foot, gazing at her father, waiting for him to say something. He looked… Well, it was very difficult to say if John Thompson could ever really be surprised. In his line of work, he had seen it all, heard it all. While Protestants weren't much for confession, people often used him as a confessional, she knew.

Still, he looked a little surprised to be in this situation.

She searched his face for signs of disappointment. That was her deepest fear. That he would be disappointed in her. Because she had tried, she really had, to be the child Ace wasn't.

Except, as she stood there, she realized that was a steaming pile of bull-pucky. Her behavior wasn't about being what Ace hadn't been. It was all about desperately wanting to please people while at the same time wishing there was a way to please herself. And the fact of the matter was, she couldn't have both those things. Not always.

That contradiction was why she had been hell-bent on running away, less because she wanted to experience the wonders of the world and more because she wanted to go off and do what she wanted without disappointing anyone.

"Jonathan isn't just my boss," she said to her dad. "He's my… Well, I don't really know. But… you know." Her throat tightened, tears burning behind her eyes.

Yes, she wanted to admit to the relationship, and she wanted to live out in the open, but that didn't make the transition from good girl to her own woman any easier.

She wanted to beg her dad for his approval. He wasn't a judgmental man, her father, but he had certainly raised her in a specific fashion, and this was not it. So while he might not condemn her, she knew she wasn't going to get his wholesale approval.

And she would have to live with that.

Living without his approval was hard. Much harder than she had thought it might be. Especially given the fact that she thought she'd accepted it just a few moments ago. But being willing to experience disapproval and truly accepting it were apparently two different things.

"Why don't you have a seat, Hayley," her father said slowly.

"No, thank you," she replied. "I'm going to stand, because if I sit down… Well, I don't know. I have too much energy to sit down. But I—I care about him." She turned to Jonathan. "I care about you. I really do. I'm so sorry I made you feel like you were a dirty secret. Like I was ashamed of you. Because any woman would be proud to be involved with you." She took a deep breath and looked around the coffee shop. "I'm dating him," she said, pointing at Jonathan. "Just so you all know."

"Hayley," her father said, standing up, "come to dinner this week."

"With him?"

"If you want to. But please know that we want to know about your life. Even if it isn't what we would choose for you, we want to know." He didn't mean Jonathan specifically. He meant being in a physical relationship without the benefit of any kind of commitment, much less marriage.

But the way he looked at her, with nothing but love, made her ache all over. Made her throat feel so tight she could scarcely breathe.

She felt miserable. And she felt strong. She wasn't sure which emotion was more prominent. She had seen her father look at Ace like this countless times, had seen him talk about her brother with a similar expression on his face. Her father was loving, and he was as supportive as he could be, but he also had hard lines.

"I guess we'll see," she said.

"I suppose. I also imagine you need to have a talk with him," he said, tilting his head toward Jonathan, who was looking uncertain. She'd never seen Jonathan look uncertain before.

"Oh," she said, "I imagine I do."

"Come home if you need anything."

For some reason, she suddenly became aware of the tension in her father's expression. He was the pastor of Copper Ridge. And the entire town was watching him. So whether he wanted to or not, he couldn't haul off and punch Jonathan. He couldn't yell at her—though he never had yelled in all her life. And he was leaving her to sort out her own circumstances, when she could feel that he very much wanted to stay and sort them out for her.

Maybe Jonathan was right. Maybe she had never put a foot out of line because the rules were easier. There were no rules to what she was doing now, and no one was going to step in and tell her what to do. No one was going to pull her back if she went too far. Not even her father. Maybe that had been her real issue with taking this relationship public. Not so much the disappointment as the loss of a safety net.

Right now, Hayley felt like she was standing on the edge of an abyss. She had no idea how far she might fall, how bad it might hurt when she landed. If she would even survive it.

She was out here, living her potential mistakes, standing on the edge of a lot of potential pain.

Because with the barrier of following the rules removed, with no need to leave to experience things… Well, it was just her. Her heart and what she felt for Jonathan.

There was nothing in the way. No excuses. No false idea that this could never be anything, because she was leaving in the end.

As her father walked out of the coffeehouse, taking with him an entire truckload of her excuses, she realized exactly what she had been protecting herself from.

Falling in love. With Jonathan. With a man who might never love her back. Wanting more, wanting everything, with the man least likely to give it to her.

She had been hiding behind the secretary desk at the church, listening to everybody else's problems, without ever incurring any of her own. She had witnessed a whole lot of heartbreak, a whole lot of struggle, but she had always been removed from it.

She didn't want to protect herself from this. She didn't want to hide.

"Why did you do that?" Jonathan asked.

"Because you were mad at me yesterday. I hurt your feelings."

He laughed, a dark, humorless sound. "Hayley," he said, "I don't exactly have feelings to hurt."

"That's not true," she said. "I know you do."

"Honey, that stuff was beaten out of me by my father before I was five years old. And whatever was left... It pretty much dissolved when my mother walked away and left me with a wounded sister to care for. That stuff just kind of leaves you numb. All you can do is survive. Work on through life as hard as you can, worry about putting food on the table. Worry about trying to do right by a kid who's had every unfair thing come down on her. You think you being embarrassed to hold my hand in public is going to hurt my feelings after that?"

She hated when he did this. When he drew lines between their levels of experience and made her feel silly.

She closed the distance between them and put her fingertips on his shoulder. Then she leaned in and kissed him, in full view of everybody in the coffeehouse. He put his hand on her hip, and even though he didn't enthusiastically kiss her back, he made no move to end it, either.

"Why do I get the feeling you are a little embarrassed to be with *me*?" she asked, when she pulled away from him.

He arched his brow. "I'm not embarrassed to be with you."

Maybe he wasn't. But there was something bothering him. "You're upset because everyone knows. And now there will be consequences if you do something to hurt me."

"When," he said, his tone uncompromising. "*When* I do something. That's what everyone is thinking. Trust me, Hayley, they don't think for one second that this might end in some fairy-tale wedding bullshit."

Hayley jerked back, trying to fight the feeling

that she had just been slapped in the face. For whatever reason, he was trying to elicit exactly that response, and she really didn't want to give it to him. "Fine. Maybe that is what they think. But why does it matter? That's the question, isn't it? Why does what other people think matter more than what you or I might want?

"You were right about me. My choices were less about what other people might think, and more about what might happen to me if I found out I had never actually been reined in." She shook her head. "If I discovered that all along I could have done exactly what I wanted to, with no limit on it. Before now, I never took the chance to find out who I was. I was happy to be told. And I think I've been a little afraid of who I might be beneath all of these expectations."

"Why? Because you might harbor secret fantasies of shoplifting doilies out of the Trading Post?"

"No," Hayley said, "because I might go and get myself hurt. If I had continued working at the church, if I'd kept on gazing at the kind of men I met there from across the room, never making a move because waiting for them to do it was right, pushing down all of my desires because it was lust I shouldn't feel… I would have been safe. I wouldn't be sitting here in this coffee shop with you, shaking because I'm scared, because I'm a little bit turned on thinking about what we did last night."

"I understand the turned on part," he said, his

voice rough like gravel. He lifted his hand, dragging his thumb over her lower lip. "Why are you afraid?"

"I'm afraid because just like you said… There's a very low chance of this ending in some fairy-tale wedding…nonsense. And I want all of that." Her chest seized tight, her throat closing up to a painful degree. "With you. If you were wondering. And that is… That's so scary. Because I knew you would look at me like that if I told you."

His face was flat, his dark eyes blazing. He was… well, he was angry, rather than indifferent. Somehow, she had known he would be.

"You shouldn't be afraid of not getting your fairy tale with me. If anything, you should be relieved. Nobody wants to stay with me for the rest of their life, Hayley, trust me. You're supposed to go to Paris. And you're going to Paris."

"I don't want to go," she said, because she wanted to stay here, with him. Or take him with her. But she didn't want to be without him.

"Dammit," he said, his voice like ground-up glass. "Hayley, you're not going to change your plans because of me. That would last how long? Maybe a year? Maybe two if you're really dedicated. But I know exactly how that ends—with you deciding you would rather be anywhere but stuck in my house, stuck in this town."

"But I don't feel stuck. I never did. It was all… me being afraid. But the thing is, Jonathan, I never

wanted anything more than I wanted my safety.
Thinking I needed to escape was just a response to
this missing piece inside of me that I couldn't put a
name to. But I know what it is now."

"Don't," he bit out.

"It was you," she said. "All of this time it was you.
Don't you see? I never wanted anyone or anything
badly enough to take the chance. To take the risk.
To expose myself, to step out of line. But you... I
do want you that badly."

"Because you were forced to take the risk. You
had to own it. Yesterday, you didn't have to, and
so you didn't. You pulled away from me when we
walked down the street, didn't want anyone to see."

"That wasn't about you. It was about me. It was
about the fact that...basically, everybody in town
knows I've never dated anybody. So in my case it's
a little bit like announcing that I lost my virginity,
and it's embarrassing."

Except now she was having this conversation with
him in a coffeehouse, where people she knew were
sitting only a few feet away, undoubtedly straining
to hear her over the sound of the espresso machine.
But whatever. She didn't care. For the first time in
her life, she really, really didn't care. She cared about
him. She cared about this relationship. About doing
whatever she needed to do to make him see that
everything she was saying was true.

"I'm over it," she added. "I just had to decide that

I was. Well, now I have. Because it doesn't get any more horrifying than having to admit that you were having your first affair to your father."

"You see," he said. "I wouldn't know. Nobody was all that invested in me when I lost my virginity, or why. I was fifteen, if you were curious. So forgive me if your concerns seem foreign to me. It's just that I know how this all plays out. People say they love you, then they punch you in the face. You take care of somebody all of their damn life, and then they take off with the one person you spent all that time protecting them from. Yeah, they say they love you, and then they leave. That's life."

Hayley's chest tightened, her heart squeezing painfully. "I didn't say I loved you."

He looked stricken by that. "Well, good. At least you didn't lie to me."

She did love him, though. But he had introduced the word. Love and its effects were clearly the things that scared him most about what was happening between them.

Love loomed large between them. Love was clearly on the table here. Even if he didn't want it to be, there it was. Even if he was going to deny it, there it was.

Already in his mind, in his heart, whether she said it or not.

She opened her mouth to say it, but it stuck in her throat.

Because he had already decided it would be a lie

if she spoke the words. He was so dedicated to that idea. To his story about who Jonathan Bear was, and who he had to be, and how people treated him. His behavior was so very close to what she had been doing for so long.

"Jonathan—"

He cut her off. "I don't love people," he said. "You know what I love? I love things. I love my house. I love my money. I love that company that I've spent so many hours investing in. I love the fact that I own a mountain, and can ride a horse from one end of my land to the other, and get a sense of everything that can never be taken from me. But I'll never love another person, not again." He stood up, gripping her chin with his thumb and forefinger. "Not even you. Because I will never love anything I can't buy right back, do you understand?"

She nodded, swallowing hard. "Yes," she said.

His pain was hemorrhaging from him, bleeding out of every pore, and there was nothing she could do to stop it. He was made of fury, of rage, and he was made of hurt, whether he would admit it or not.

"I think we're done then, Hayley."

He moved away from her, crossing the coffee-house and walking out the door. Every eye in the room was on her, everybody watching to see what she would do next. So she did the only thing she could.

She stood up and she ran after Jonathan Bear for the entire town to see.

* * *

Jonathan strode down the street. The heavy gray sky was starting to crack, raindrops falling onto his head. His shoulders. Good. That was just about perfect.

It took him a few more strides to realize he was headed away from his car, but he couldn't think clearly enough to really grasp where he was going. His head was pounding like horse hooves over the grass, and he couldn't grab hold of a thought to save his life.

"Jonathan!"

He turned, looking down the mostly empty street, to see Hayley running after him, her dark hair flying behind her, rain flying into her face. She was making a spectacle of herself, right here on Main, and she didn't seem to care at all. Something about that made him feel like he'd been turned to stone, rooted to the spot, his heart thundering heavily in his chest.

"Don't run from me," she said, coming to a stop in front of him, breathing hard. "Don't run from us."

"You're the one who's running, honey," he said, keeping his voice deliberately flat.

"We're not done," she said. "We're not going to be done just because you say so. You might be the boss at your house, but you're not the boss here." Her words were jumbled up, fierce and ferocious. "What about what I want?"

He gritted his teeth. "Well, the problem is you

made the mistake of assuming I might care what you want."

She sprang forward, pounding a closed fist on his shoulder. The gesture was so aggressive, so very unlike Hayley that it immobilized him. "You do care. You're not a mountain, you're just a man, and you do care. But you're awfully desperate to prove that you don't. You're awfully desperate to prove you have no worth. And I have to wonder why that is."

"I don't have to prove it. Everyone who's ever wandered through my life has proved it, Hayley. You're a little bit late to this party. You're hardly going to take thirty-five years of neglect and make me feel differently about it. Make me come to different conclusions than I've spent the past three decades drawing."

"Why not?" she asked. "That's kind of the point of knowing someone. Of being with them. They change you. You've certainly changed me. You made me…well, more me than I've ever been."

"I never said I needed to change."

"That's ridiculous. Of course you need to change. You live in that big house all by yourself, you're angry at your sister because she figured out how to let something go when you can't. And you're about ready to blow this up—to blow us up—to keep yourself safe." She shivered, the rain making dark spots on her top, drops rolling down her face.

"There's no reason any of this has to end, Hayley." He gritted his teeth, fighting against the slow, expanding feeling growing in his chest, fighting against the pain starting to push against the back of his eyes. "But you have to accept what I'm willing to give. And it may not be what you want, what you're looking for. If it's not, if that makes you leave, then you're no different from anyone else who's ever come through my life, and you won't be any surprise to me."

Hayley looked stricken by that, pale. And he could see her carefully considering her words. "Wow. That's a very smart way to build yourself an impenetrable fort there, Jonathan. How can anyone demand something of you, if you're determined to equate high expectations with the people who abandoned you? If you're determined to believe that someone asking anything of you is the same as not loving you at all?"

"You haven't said you loved me." His voice was deliberately hard. He didn't know why he was bringing that up again. Didn't know why he was suspended between the desire for her to tell him she didn't, and the need—the intense, soul-shattering need—to hear her say it, even if he could never accept it. Even if he could never return it.

"My mistake," she said, her voice thin. "What will you do if I tell you, Jonathan? Will you say it doesn't matter, that it isn't real? Because you know everything, don't you? Even my heart."

"I know more about the world than you do, little girl," he said, his throat feeling tight for some reason. "Whatever your intentions, I have a better idea of what the actual outcome might be."

She shocked him by taking two steps forward, eliminating the air between them, pressing her hand against his chest. His heart raged beneath her touch, and he had a feeling she could tell.

"I love you." She stared at him for a moment, then she stretched up on her toes and pressed a kiss to his lips. Her lips were slick and cold from the rain, and he wanted to consume her. Wanted to pretend that words didn't matter. That there was nothing but this kiss.

For a moment, a heartbeat, he pretended that was true.

"I love you," she said again, when they parted. "But that doesn't mean I won't expect something from you. In fact, that would be pretty sorry love if I expected to come into your life and change nothing, mean nothing. I want you to love me back, Jonathan. I want you to open yourself up. I want you to let me in. I want you to be brave."

He grabbed hold of her arms, held her against his chest. He didn't give a damn who might see them. "You're telling me to be brave? What have you ever faced down that scared you? Tell me, Hayley."

"You," she said breathlessly.

He released his hold on her and took a step back,

swearing violently. "All the more reason you should walk away, I expect."

"Do you know why you scare me, Jonathan? You make me want something I can't control. You make me want something I can't predict. There are no rules for this. There is no safety. Loving you… I have no guarantees. There is no neat map for how this might work out. It's not a math equation, where I can add doing the right things with saying the right things and make you change. You have to decide. You have to choose this. You have to choose us. The rewards for being afraid, or being good, aren't worth as much as the reward for being brave. So I'm going to be brave.

"I love you. And I want you to love me back. I want you to take a chance—on me."

She was gazing at him, her eyes blazing with light and intensity. How long would it take for that light to dim? How long would it take for him to kill it? How long would it take for her to decide—like everyone else in his life—that he wasn't worth the effort?

It was inevitable. That was how it always ended.

"No," he said, the word scraping his throat raw as it escaped.

"No?" The devastation in her voice cut him like a knife.

"No. But hey, one more for your list," he said, hating himself with every syllable.

"What?"

"You got your kiss in the rain. I did a lot for you, checked off a lot of your boxes. Go find some other man to fill in the rest."

Then he turned and left her standing in the street.

And in front of God and everybody, Jonathan Bear walked away from Hayley Thompson, and left whatever remained of his heart behind with her.

Thirteen

This was hell. Perhaps even literally. Hayley had wondered about hell a few times, growing up the daughter of a pastor. Now, she thought that if hell were simply living with a broken heart, with the rejection of the person you loved more than anything else echoing in your ears, it would be pretty effective eternal damnation.

She was lying on her couch, tears streaming down her face. She was miserable, and she didn't even want to do anything about it. She just wanted to sit in it.

Oh, she had been so cavalier about the pain that would come when Jonathan ended things. Back in the beginning, when she had been justifying losing her virginity to him, she had been free and easy about the possibility of heartbreak.

But she hadn't loved him then. So she really hadn't known.

Hadn't known that it would be like shards of glass digging into her chest every time she took a breath. Hadn't known that it was actual, physical pain. That her head would throb and her eyes would feel like sandpaper from all the crying.

That her body, and her soul, would feel like they had been twisted, wrung out and draped over a wire to dry in the brutal, unfeeling coastal air.

This was the experience he had talked about. The one that wasn't worth having.

She rolled onto her back, thinking over the past weeks with Jonathan. Going to his house, getting her first job away from the church. How nervous she had been. How fluttery she had felt around him.

Strangely, she felt her lips curve into a smile.

It was hard to reconcile the woman she was now with the girl who had first knocked on his door for that job interview.

She hadn't even realized what all that fluttering meant. What the tightening in her nipples, the pressure between her thighs had meant. She knew now. Desire. Need. Things she would associate with Jonathan for the rest of her life, no matter where she went, no matter who else she might be with.

He'd told her to find someone else.

Right now, the idea of being with another man made her cringe.

She wasn't ready to think about that. She was too raw. And she still wanted him. Only him.

Jonathan was more than an experience.

He had wrenched her open. Pulled her out of the safe space she'd spent so many years hiding in. He had shown her a love that was bigger than fear.

Unfortunately, because that love was so big, the desolation of it was crippling.

She sat up, scrubbing her arm over her eyes. She needed to figure out what she was going to do next.

Something had crystallized for her earlier today, during the encounter with Jonathan and her father. She didn't need to run away. She didn't need to leave town, or gain anonymity, in order to have what she wanted. To be who she wanted.

She didn't need to be the church secretary, didn't need to be perfect or hide what she was doing. She could still go to her father's church on Sunday, and go to dinner at her parents' house on Sunday evening.

She didn't have to abandon her home, her family, her faith. Sure, it might be uncomfortable to unite her family and her need to find herself, but if there was one thing loving Jonathan had taught her, it was that sometimes uncomfortable was worth it.

She wasn't going to let heartbreak stop her.

She thought back to how he had looked at her

earlier today, those black eyes impassive as he told her he wouldn't love her back.

Part of her wanted to believe she was right about him. That he was afraid. That he was protecting himself.

Another part of her felt that was a little too hopeful. Maybe that gorgeous, experienced man simply couldn't love his recently-a-virgin assistant.

Except…she had been so certain, during a few small moments, that she had given something to him, too. Just like he had given so much to her.

For some reason, he was dedicated to the idea that nobody stayed. That people looked at him and saw the worst. She couldn't understand why he would find that comforting, and yet a part of him must.

It made her ache. Her heart wasn't broken only for her, but for him, too. For all the love he wouldn't allow himself to accept.

She shook her head. Later. Later she would feel sorry for him. Right now, she was going to wallow in her own pain.

Because at the end of the day, Jonathan had made the choice to turn away from her, to turn away from love.

Right now, she would feel sorry for herself. Then maybe she would plan a trip to Paris.

"Do you want to invite me in?"

Jonathan looked at his sister, standing on the porch, looking deceptively calm.

"Do I have a choice?"

Rebecca shook her head, her long dark hair swinging behind her like a curtain. "Not really. I didn't drive all the way out here to have this conversation with moths buzzing around me."

It was dark out, and just as Rebecca had said, there were bugs fluttering around the porch light near her face.

"Come in, then," he said, moving aside.

She blinked when she stepped over the threshold, a soft smile touching her lips. The scar tissue on the left side of her mouth pulled slightly. Scar tissue that had been given to her by the man she was going to marry. Oh, it had been an accident, and Jonathan knew it. But with all the pain and suffering the accident had caused Rebecca, intent had never much mattered to him.

"This is beautiful, Jonathan," she said, her dark eyes flickering to him. "I haven't been here since it was finished."

He shrugged. "Well, that was your choice."

"You don't like my fiancé. And you haven't made much of an effort to change that. I don't know what you expect from me."

"Appreciation, maybe, for all the years I spent taking care of you?" He wanted to cut his own balls off for saying that. Basically, right about now he wanted to escape his own skin. He was a bastard. Even he thought so.

He was sitting in his misery now, existing fully in the knowledge of the pain he had caused Hayley.

He should never have had that much power over her. He never should have touched her. This misery was the only possible way it could have turned out. His only real defense was that he hadn't imagined a woman like Hayley would ever fall in love with a man like him.

"Right. Because we've never had that discussion."

His sister's tone was dry, and he could tell she was pretty unimpressed with him. Well, fair enough. He was unimpressed with himself.

"I still don't understand why you love him, Rebecca. I really don't."

"What is love to you, Jonathan?"

An image of Hayley's face swam before his mind's eye. "What the hell kind of question is that?"

"A relevant one," she said. "I think. Particularly when we get down to why exactly I'm here. Congratulations. After spending most of your life avoiding being part of the rumor mill, you're officially hot small-town gossip."

"Am I?" He wasn't very surprised to hear that.

"Something about kissing the pastor's daughter on Main Street in the rain. And having a fight with her."

"That's accurate."

"What's going on?"

"What it looks like. I was sleeping with her. We had a fight. Now we're not sleeping together."

Rebecca tilted her head to the side. "I feel like I'm missing some information."

"Hayley was working for me—I assume you knew that."

"Vaguely," she said, her eyes glittering with curiosity.

"And I'm an asshole. So when I found out my assistant was a virgin, I figured I would help her with that." It was a lie, but one he was comfortable with. He was comfortable painting himself as the villain. Everybody would, anyway. So why not add his own embellishment to the tale.

"Right," Rebecca said, sarcasm dripping from her voice. "Because you're a known seducer of innocent women."

Jonathan turned away, running his hand over his hair. "I'm not the nicest guy, Rebecca. We all know that."

"I know *you* think that," Rebecca said. "And I know we've had our differences. But when I needed you, you were there for me. Always. Even when Gage broke my heart, and you couldn't understand why it mattered, why I wanted to be with him, in the end, you supported me. Always. Every day of my life. I don't even remember my father. I remember you. You taught me how to ride a bike, how to ride a horse. You fought for me, tirelessly. Worked for me. You don't think I don't know how tired you were? How much you put into making our home...a home?

Bad men don't do that. Bad men hit their wives, hit their children. Abandon their daughters. Our fathers were bad men, Jonathan. But you never were."

Something about those words struck him square in the chest. Their fathers *were* bad men.

He had always known that.

But he had always believed somewhere deep down that he must be bad, too. Not because he thought being an abusive bastard was hereditary. But because if his father had beaten him, and his mother had left him, there must be something about him that was bad.

Something visible. Something that the whole town could see.

He thought back to all the kindness on Pastor John Thompson's face, kindness Jonathan certainly hadn't deserved from the old man when he was doing his absolute damnedest to start a fight in the middle of The Grind.

He had been so determined to have John confirm that Jonathan was bad. That he was wrong.

Because there was something freeing about the anger that belief created deep inside his soul.

It had been fuel. All his life that belief had been his fuel. Gave him something to fight against. Something to be angry about.

An excuse to never get close to anyone.

Because underneath all the anger was nothing but despair. Despair because his parents had left him, because they couldn't love him enough. Because he wasn't worth…anything.

His need for love had never gone away, but he'd shoved it down deep. Easier to do when you had convinced yourself you could never have it.

He looked at Rebecca and realized he had despaired over her, too. When she had chosen Gage. Jonathan had decided it was just one more person who loved him and didn't want to stay.

Yeah, it was much easier, much less painful to believe that he was bad. Because it let him keep his distance from the pain. Because it meant he didn't have to try.

"What do you think love is?" Rebecca asked again, more persistent this time.

He didn't have an answer. Not one with words. All he had were images, feelings. Watching Rebecca sleep after a particularly hard day. Praying child services wouldn't come by to check on her while he was at work, and find her alone and him negligent.

And Hayley. Her soft hands on his body, her sweet surrender. The trust it represented. The way she made him feel. Like he was on fire, burning up from the inside out. Like he could happily stay for the rest of his life in a one-room cabin, without any of the money or power he had acquired over the past few years, and be perfectly content.

The problem was, he couldn't make her stay with him.

This house, his company, those things were his. In a way that Hayley could never be. In a way that no one ever could be.

People were always able to leave.

He felt like a petulant child even having that thought. But he didn't know how the hell else he could feel secure. And he didn't think he could stand having another person walk away.

"I don't know," he said.

Rebecca shook her head, her expression sad. "That's a damn shame, Jonathan, because you show me love all the time. Whether you know what to call it or not, you've given it to me tirelessly over the years, and without you, without it, I don't know where I would be. You stayed with me when everybody else left."

"But who stayed with me?" he asked, feeling like an ass for even voicing that question. "You had to stay. I had to take care of you. But the minute you could go out on your own you did."

"Because that's what your love did for me, you idiot."

"Not very well. Because you were always worried I thought of you as a burden, weren't you? It almost ruined your relationship with Gage, if I recall correctly."

"Yes," she said, "but that wasn't about you. That was my baggage. And you did everything in your power to help me, even when you knew the result would be me going back to Gage. That's love, Jonathan." She shook her head. "I love you, too. I love you enough to want you to have your own life, one that doesn't revolve around taking care of me. That doesn't revolve around what happened to us in the past."

He looked around the room, at the house that meant so much to him. A symbol of security, of his ability to care for Rebecca, if her relationship went to hell. And he realized that creating this security for her somehow enabled him to deny his own weaknesses. His own fears.

This house had only ever been for him. A fortress to barricade himself in.

Wasn't that what Hayley had accused him of? Building himself a perfect fortress to hide in?

If everybody hated him, he didn't have to try. If there was something wrong with him, he never had to do what was right. If all he loved were things, he never had to risk loss.

They were lies. Lies he told himself because he was a coward.

And it had taken a virginal church secretary to uncover the truth.

She had stood in front of him and said she wanted love more than she wanted to be safe. And he had turned her down.

He was afraid. Had been all his life. But before this very moment, he would have rather cut out his own heart than admit it.

But now, standing with his sister looking at him

like he was the saddest damn thing she'd ever seen, a hole opened in his chest. A hole Hayley had filled.

"But doesn't it scare you?" he asked, his voice rough. "What if he leaves?"

She reached out, putting her hand on his. "It would break my heart. But I would be okay. I would have you. And I would…still be more whole than I was before I loved him. That's the thing about love. It doesn't make you weak, Jonathan, it makes you stronger. Opening yourself up, letting people in… that makes your life bigger. It makes your life richer. Maybe it's a cliché, but from where I'm standing you need to hear the cliché. You need to start believing it."

"I don't understand why she would want to be with me," Jonathan said. "She's…sweet. And she's never been hurt. I'm…well, I'm a mess. That's not what she deserves. She deserves to have a man who's in mint condition, like she is."

"But that's not how love works. If love made sense, if it was perfectly fair, then Gage West would not have been the man for me. He was the last man on earth I should have wanted, Jonathan. Nobody knows that more than me, and him. It took a miracle for me to let go of all my anger and love him. At the same time… I couldn't help myself.

"Love is strange that way. You fall into it whether you want to or not. Then the real fight is figuring out how to live it. How to become the person you need to be so you can hold on to that love. But I'm willing to bet you are the man she needs. Not some mint condition, new-in-the-box guy. But a strong man who has proved, time and time again, that no matter how hard life is, no matter how intensely the storm rages, he'll be there for you. And more than that, he'll throw his body over yours to protect you if it comes to that. That's what I see when I look at you, Jonathan. What's it going to take for you to see that in yourself?"

"I don't think I'm ever going to," he said slowly, imagining Hayley again, picturing her as she stared up at him on the street. Fury, hurt, love shining from her eyes. "But...if she sees it..."

"That's a start," Rebecca said. "As long as you don't let her get away. As long as you don't push her away."

"It's too late for that. She's probably not going to want to see me again. She's probably not going to want me back."

"Well, you won't know unless you ask." Rebecca took a deep breath. "The best thing about love is it has the capacity to forgive on a pretty incredible level. But if there's one thing you and I both know, it's that it's hard to forgive someone leaving. Don't make that the story. Go back. Ask for forgiveness. Change what needs to be changed. Mostly...love her. The rest kind of takes care of itself."

Fourteen

Hayley had just settled back onto her couch for more quality sitting and weeping when she heard a knock at her door.

She stood up, brushing potato chip crumbs off her pajamas and grimacing. Maybe it was Cassie, bringing up baked goods. The other woman had done that earlier; maybe now she was bringing more. Hayley could only hope.

She had a gaping wound in her chest that could be only temporarily soothed by butter.

Without bothering to fix her hair—which was on top of her head in a messy knot—she jerked the door open.

And there he was. Dark eyes glittering, gorgeous

mouth pressed into a thin line. His dark hair tied back low on his neck, the way she was accustomed to seeing him during the day.

Her heart lurched up into her throat, trying to make a break for it.

She hadn't been expecting him, but she imagined expecting him wouldn't have helped. Jonathan Bear wasn't someone you could anticipate.

"What are you doing here?"

He looked around. "I came here to talk to you. Were you…expecting someone else?"

"Yes. A French male prostitute." He lifted his brows. "Well, you told me to find another man to tick my boxes."

"I think you mean a gigolo."

"I don't know what they're called," she said, exasperated.

The corner of his mouth twitched. "Well, I promise to be quick. I won't interrupt your sex date."

She stepped to the side, ignoring the way her whole body hurt as she did. "I don't have a sex date." She cleared her throat. "Just so you know."

"Somehow, I didn't think you did."

"You don't know me," she grumbled, turning away from him, pressing her hand to her chest to see if her heart was beating as hard and fast as she felt like it was.

It was.

"I do, Hayley. I know you pretty damn well. Maybe

better than I know myself. And…I think you might know me better than I know myself, too." He sounded different. Sad. Tired.

She turned around to face him, and with his expression more fully illuminated by the light, she saw weariness written there. Exhaustion.

"For all the good it did me," she said, crossing her arms tightly in a bid to protect herself. Really, though, it was too late. There wasn't anything left to protect. He had shattered her irrevocably.

"Yeah, well. It did me a hell of a lot of good. At least, I hope it's going to. I hope I'm not too late."

"Too late for what? To stick the knife in again or…?"

"To tell you I love you," he said.

Everything froze inside her. Absolutely everything. The air in her lungs, her heart, the blood in her veins.

"You…you just said… Don't tease me, Jonathan. Don't play with me. I know I'm younger than you. I know that I'm innocent. But if you came back here to lie to me, to say what you think I need to hear so you can…keep having me in your bed, or whatever—"

Suddenly, she found herself being hauled forward into his arms, against his chest. "I do want you in my bed," he said, "make no mistake about that. But sex is just sex, Hayley, even when it's good. And what we have is good.

"But here's something you don't know, because

you don't have experience with it. Sex isn't love. And it doesn't feel like this. I feel…like everything in me is broken and stronger at the same time, and I don't know how in the hell that can be true. And when you told me you loved me… I knew I could either let go of everything in the past or hold on to it harder to protect myself." He shook his head. "I protected myself."

"Yeah, well. What about protecting me?"

"I thought maybe I was protecting you, too. But it's all tangled up in this big lie that I've been telling myself for years. I told you I didn't love people, that I love things. But I said that only because I've had way too much experience with people I love leaving. A house can't walk away, Hayley. A mountain can't up and abandon you. But you could.

"One day, you could wake up and regret that you tied your future to me. When you could have done better… When you could have had a man who wasn't so damn broken." He cupped her cheek, bent down and kissed her lips. "What did I do to earn the love of someone like you? Someone so beautiful…so soft. You're everything I'm not, Hayley Thompson, and all the reasons I love you make perfect sense to me. But why do you love me? That's what I can't quite figure out."

Hayley looked into his eyes, so full of pain, so deeply wounded. She would have never thought a man like him would need reassurance from anyone, least of all a woman like her.

"I know I don't have a lot of experience, Jonathan. Well, any experience apart from you. I know that I haven't seen the whole world. I haven't even seen the whole state. But I've seen your heart. The kind of man you are. The change that knowing you, loving you, created in me. And I know...perfect love casts out all fear.

"I can't say I haven't been afraid these past couple of days. Afraid I couldn't be with you. That things might not work out with us. But when I stood on Main Street... I knew fear couldn't be allowed to win. It was your love that brought me to that conclusion. Your love was bigger than the fear inside me. I don't need experience to understand that. I don't need to travel the world or date other men for the sake of experience. I need you. Because whether or not you're perfect, you're perfect for me."

"*You're* perfect," he said, his voice rough. "So damned perfect. I want...to take you to Canada."

She blinked. "Well. That's not exactly an offer to run off to Vegas."

"You want to use your passport. Why wait? Let's go now. Your boss will let you off. I'm sure of it."

Something giddy bubbled up in her chest. Something wonderful. "Right now? Really?"

"Right the hell now."

"Yes," she said. "Yes, let's go to Canada."

"It's not the Eiffel Tower," he said, "but I will take you there someday. I promise you that."

"The only thing I need is you," she said. "The rest is negotiable."

His lips crashed down on hers, his kiss desperate and intense, saying the deep, poetic things she doubted her stoic cowboy would ever say out loud. But that was okay. The kiss said plenty all on its own.

Epilogue

Jonathan hated wearing a suit. He'd never done it before, but he had come to a swift and decisive conclusion the moment he'd finished doing up his tie.

Hayley was standing in their bedroom, looking amused. The ring on her left hand glittered as bright as her eyes, and suddenly, it wasn't the tie that was strangling him. It was just her. The love on her beautiful face. The fact she loved him.

He still hadn't quite figured out why. Still wasn't sure he saw all the things in himself that Rebecca had spoken of that day, all the things Hayley talked about when she said she loved him.

But Hayley did love him. And that was a gift he cherished.

"You're not going to make me wear a suit when we do this, are you?" he asked.

"I might," she said. "You look really hot in a suit."

He wrapped his arm around her waist and pulled her to his chest. "You look hottest in nothing at all. Think we could compromise?"

"We've created enough scandal already without me showing up naked to my wedding. Anyway, I'm wearing white. I am a traditional girl, after all."

"Honey, you oughta wear red."

"Are you calling me a scarlet woman?"

He nodded. "Yes, and I think you proved your status earlier this morning."

She blushed. She still blushed, even after being with him for six months. Blushed in bed, when he whispered dirty things into her ear. He loved it.

He loved *her*.

He couldn't wait to be her husband, and that was something he hadn't imagined ever feeling. Looking forward to being a husband.

Of course, he was looking forward to the honeymoon even more. To staying in a little apartment in Paris with a view of the Eiffel Tower.

For him, trading in a view of the mountains for a view of the city didn't hold much appeal. But she wanted it. And the joy he got from giving Hayley what she wanted was the biggest thing in his world.

Waiting to surprise her with the trip was damn near killing him.

"You have to hurry," she said, pushing at his shoulder. "You're giving the bride away, after all."

Jonathan took a deep breath. Yeah, it was time. Time to give his sister to that Gage West, who would never deserve her, but who loved her, so Jonathan was willing to let it go. Willing to give them his blessing.

Actually, over the past few months he'd gotten kind of attached to the bastard who would be his brother-in-law. Something he'd thought would never be possible only a little while ago.

But love changed you. Rebecca had been right about that.

"All right," he said. "Let's go then."

Hayley kissed his cheek and took his hand, leading him out of the bedroom and down the stairs. The wedding guests were out on the back lawn, waiting for the event to start. When he and Hayley exited the house, they all turned to look.

He and Hayley still turned heads, and he had a feeling they always would.

Jonathan Bear had always been seen as a bad boy. In all the ways that phrase applied. The kind of boy no parent wanted their daughter to bring home to Sunday dinner. And yet the pastor's daughter had.

He'd definitely started out that way. But somehow, through some miracle, he'd earned the love of a good woman.

And because of her love, he was determined to be the best man he could possibly be.

* * * * *

She had to calm down.

She was going to see Jaeger again. Her onetime lover, the father of her child, the man she'd spent the past eighteen months fantasizing about. In Milan she hadn't been able to look at him without wanting to kiss him, without wanting to get naked with him as soon as humanly possible.

Jaeger, the same man who'd blocked her from his life.

She had to pull herself together! She was not a gauche girl about to meet her first crush. She had sapphires to sell, her house to save, a child to raise.

Piper turned when male voices drifted toward her, and she immediately recognized Jaeger's deep timbre. Her skin prickled and burned and her heart flew out of her chest.

"Miss Mills?"

His hair was slightly shorter, she noticed, his stubble a little heavier. His eyes were still the same arresting blue, but his shoulders seemed broader, his arms under the sleeves of the black oxford shirt more defined. A soft leather belt was threaded through the loops of black chinos.

The corner of his mouth tipped up, the same way it had the first time they'd met, and like before, the butterflies in her stomach crashed into one another. She couldn't, wouldn't throw herself into his arms and tell him that her mouth had missed his, that her body still craved his.

He held out his hand. "I'm Jaeger Ballantyne."

Yes, I know. We did several things to each other that, when I remember Milan, still make me blush.

What had she said in Italy? *When we meet again, we'll pretend we never saw each other naked.*

Was he really going to take her statement literally?

Jaeger shoved his hand into the pocket of his pants and rocked on his heels, his expression wary. "Okay, skipping the pleasantries. I understand you have some sapphires you'd like me to see?"

His words instantly reminded her of her mission. She'd spent one night with the Playboy of Park Avenue and he'd unknowingly given her the best gift of her life, but that wasn't why she was here. She needed him to buy the gems so she could keep her house.

Piper nodded. "Right. Yes, I have sapphires."

"I only deal in exceptional stones, Ms. Mills."

Piper reached into the side pocket of her tote bag and hauled out a knuckle-size cut sapphire. "This exceptional enough for you, Ballantyne?"

*Don't miss
HIS EX'S WELL KEPT SECRET by Joss Wood,
available April 2017 wherever
Harlequin® Desire books and ebooks are sold.*

*And follow the rest of the Ballantynes with
REUNITED…AND PREGNANT, available June 2017,
Linc's story, available August 2017,
and Sage's story, available January 2018.*

www.Harlequin.com

TEN-DAY BABY TAKEOVER
BY KAREN BOOTH,

PART OF HARLEQUIN DESIRE'S
#1 BESTSELLING SERIES

*Powerful men...wrapped around
their babies' little fingers.*

A BILLIONAIRE'S BABY DEAL!

One look into his infant son's trusting blue gaze
and Aiden Langford knows his wild days are over.
If only he can get Sarah Daltrey, his son's temporary
guardian, to give him daddy lessons. Certainly she'll
agree to his ten-day proposal to stay as the nanny.
He just needs to keep his mind on parenting and
off Sarah's seductive curves...

*Available April 2017 wherever
Harlequin® Desire books and ebooks are sold.*

HD83836

Whatever You're Into... Passionate Reads

Looking for more passionate reads from Harlequin®?
Fear not! Harlequin® Presents, Harlequin® Desire and
Harlequin® Blaze offer you irresistible romance stories
featuring powerful heroes.

❤HARLEQUIN® *Presents*

Do you want alpha males, decadent glamour and jet-set
lifestyles? Step into the sensational, sophisticated world of
Harlequin® Presents, where sinfully tempting heroes ignite a
fierce and wickedly irresistible passion!

❤HARLEQUIN® *Desire*

Harlequin® Desire novels are powerful, passionate and
provocative contemporary romances set against a backdrop of
wealth, privilege and sweeping family saga. Alpha heroes with
a soft side meet strong-willed but vulnerable heroines amid a
dramatic world of divided loyalties, high-stakes conflict and
intense emotion.

❤HARLEQUIN® *Blaze*

Harlequin® Blaze stories sizzle with strong heroines and
irresistible heroes playing the game of modern love and lust.
They're fun, sexy and always steamy.

Be sure to check out our full selection of books
within each series every month!

Turn your love of reading into rewards you'll love with

Harlequin My Rewards

**Join for FREE today at
www.HarlequinMyRewards.com**

Earn **FREE BOOKS** of your choice.

Experience **EXCLUSIVE OFFERS** and contests.

Enjoy **BOOK RECOMMENDATIONS**
selected just for you.

PLUS! Sign up now
and get **500** points
right away!

Earn
FREE
REWARDS
Join
Today!
HarlequinMyRewards.com

HARLEQUIN®

A *Romance* FOR EVERY MOOD™

Love the Harlequin book you just read?

Your opinion matters.

Review this book on your favorite book site, review site, blog or your own social media properties and share your opinion with other readers!

Be sure to connect with us at:
Harlequin.com/Newsletters
Facebook.com/HarlequinBooks
Twitter.com/HarlequinBooks